Marian wants a new start in life but, first, she must confront her past.

"Why did ya come, Marian?"

The words were stiff, but with anger or embarrassment, she couldn't tell. His eyes were almost black, and she wondered what kind of wounds he had inside, in his heart and emotions. Were they as bad as the wounds on his wrists?

"I. . .I wanted to tell you I forgive you."

As soon as the words were out she wanted to snatch them back. They were true, but they sounded so pompous.

Hands still in his lap, he leaned forward, his eyes mere slits. "Forgive me fer what? Lovin' ya?"

It was difficult to keep looking at him. "No. For kidnapping me and Justin's nephew and niece."

He turned his face away, but looked back in a second, and she wondered if the sheriff had heard his ragged, indrawn breath.

"I was wrong to snatch ya thet way, and I'm sorry." His voice was low, and she knew he didn't want Sheriff Tucker to hear him admit to a woman he'd committed a wrongdoing. "But, Marian, I loved ya so! I figgered if I could jest git ya away with me fer awhile, ya'd learn ta love me, too."

"I. . .I need to ask your forgiveness, also."

Surprise set him against the back of the chair so suddenly he almost tipped over. "What fer?"

"I was wrong to accept your marriage proposal. I agreed to marry you for the wrong reason."

JOANN A. GROTE returns to the Minnesota setting, where she herself grew up, in this sequel to *An Honest Love*. Like the heroine of *Rekindled Flame*, Grote seeks to serve Christ in her work. She believes that readers of novels can receive a message of salvation and encouragement from well-crafted fiction.

Books by JoAnn A. Grote

HEARTSONG PRESENTS
HP36—The Sure Promise
HP51—The Unfolding Heart
HP55—Treasure of the Heart
HP103—Love's Shining Hope
HP120—An Honest Love

Rekindled Flame

JoAnn A. Grote

A sequel to *An Honest Love*

Heartsong Presents

Dedicated to my brother, Dale Olsen,
and his wife, Sue:
Two special people with hearts
as wide as the Mississippi is long.

A note from the Author:
*I love to hear from my readers! You may write to me at
the following address:* **JoAnn A. Grote
Author Relations
P.O. Box 719
Uhrichsville, OH 44683**

ISBN 1-55748-742-1

REKINDLED FLAME

Cover illustration by Kathy Arbuckle.

PRINTED IN THE U.S.A.

author's note

The mission, or Kindergarten and Industrial Association, in *Rekindled Flame* is based on the Plymouth Kindergarten and Industrial Association. The Plymouth Congregational Church established the Bethel Mission in Minneapolis, Minnesota, in 1869, not far from the Falls of St. Anthony. The mission's services expanded quickly, and in 1883 the organization moved to a larger building. About this time the name was changed to the Plymouth Kindergarten and Industrial Association, though it was commonly referred to as the Plymouth Mission for many years.

Many aspects of the mission's work were similar to the social settlements which developed across the United States and Europe in the late 1880's and 1890's. Eventually, the Kindergarten and Industrial Association became a true social settlement, with a new building called the Pillsbury Settlement House opening in 1905.

In addition to the Bethel Mission, the church in 1890 began the Newsboys' Club, which is mentioned in *Rekindled Flame*.

The Plymouth Mission, Kindergarten and Industrial Association, Pillsbury Settlement House, and Newsboys' Club touched many lives directly with Christ's love. I wonder how many lives they are still touching, through the influences passed down through the generations?

one

Marian Ames wrinkled her nose in distaste when the hackman opened the door of the horse-drawn covered cab. She might have known it would be pouring down rain when she arrived. Thank goodness the driver was holding an open umbrella for her.

"We've arrived, miss." Impatience tinged the voice of the middle-aged driver.

Gathering the skirt of her navy blue, lightweight serge traveling suit, Marian moved to the door. At the sight of the water flowing briskly down the street, she hesitated. The hackman might have an umbrella to cover her head, but there was no such device to save her new high-buttoned kid shoes and the hems of her skirt and petticoat.

Well, there was nothing to be gained despairing about it. She might as well wade right in.

Before she could put the thought into action, strong arms swung her from the covered carriage. Instinctively she clutched the wide shoulders beneath the scratchy black wool jacket.

"Watch your skirts, miss," a pleasantly deep voice rumbled impersonally from just above her ear. "Fool driver didn't bother to put on the wheel guards."

The corner of the carriage door caught her hat. Marian grasped at it with one hand, her heart sinking when she felt the pins pull from her hair and realized it was too late to save the bonnet. A moment later she was being carried towards her aunt's front porch by the man's long, sure-footed gait.

She heard, "I'll be right back with your bags, miss," as he

set her down on the porch. *About as gently as if I were a sack of meal,* she thought.

When the man straightened and reached to touch a gloved hand to the brim of his black hat, his brown eyes held an impersonal gaze. Dismay quickly replaced the cool look. "Your hair! Did I do that?"

She couldn't stop the laugh bubbling up inside. The poor man looked like an oversized puppy caught chewing the housewife's favorite tidy. She pushed the tumbled waves of blond hair behind her shoulders. "It's quite salvageable. It's only hair, after all. Besides, it's my own fault. I'm trying a new hair style, and obviously have not mastered the art of keeping it in place."

"I was certain you were wearing a hat!"

"Oh, I was. A dear little number, too. Blue velvet with a mass of feathers in front and a large bow in back." She knew her eyes were twinkling in spite of her effort to keep her voice sober. She shouldn't tease him so. He did look properly remorseful.

"I'll retrieve it for you."

He turned toward the street and her fingertips caught his sleeve. "Please don't bother. I'm sure it's unredeemable after its dunking. It was truly an old bonnet. I never travel with a new one. Rail cars and stations are beastly on one's hats. Travel by riverboat is far more genteel."

She gave him her sweetest smile, but he frowned down at her, two creases cutting deep between his thick dark eyebrows, curiosity and confusion in his gaze.

The hackman dropped a large trunk beside them. It landed with a thud, rocking the boards slightly beneath their feet.

"Have you more bags?" the stranger asked.

"Does she hef more bags? Does a duck hef feathers?" the hackman spouted inelegantly before hurrying down the water-covered walk.

"I'll help with them." The stranger followed the burly driver whose shoulders were humped against the rain.

Marian brushed some dampness from her cloak and smiled. The stranger's chivalrous efforts to keep her dry hadn't been successful. She should be angry with him for handling her so familiarly. At the very least she should be angry over the loss of her hat, and the damage done to the hairstyle she'd worked so hard to achieve that morning before leaving River's Edge. But she was tired of being angry.

This was her new start, getting away from River's Edge with its reminders of her former fiancé, Justin Knight, and the woman he had married two days before their own scheduled wedding. Most of all, she wanted to forget the foolish way she'd acted when she'd discovered his marriage. Aunt Dorothy's invitation to spend a few months with her in Minneapolis was just what she needed: no more sly looks from neighbors, no one whispering behind his hands as she passed, a new setting, a new group of young men and women with whom to socialize.

She smiled to herself, touching one of the damp curls on her shoulder. Her hairstyle had also been part of her new life, as was the lilac fragrance she wore instead of her usual lily-of-the-valley.

New outfits were a must. First thing tomorrow she'd visit Aunt Dorothy's dressmaker and order new gowns. She already had numerous new outfits, costly and the height of fashion, but the thought of wearing them was repugnant. They belonged to her trousseau, and would only be unwelcome reminders.

The door behind her opened just before the stranger and hackman arrived with another trunk and two alligator valises. A slender woman of sixty appeared in a modest gray plaid flannel house dress beneath gently silvered hair.

"Aunt Dorothy!"

Even her wrinkles look soft above the bit of lace peeking timidly about her neck, Marian thought as she caught her petite aunt in an embrace, pressing her fresh young cheek to the older one.

Aunt Dorothy returned her hug with a strength that belied her frail appearance. "Welcome, Marian. How delightful it will be to have you here!"

Warmth spread through Marian at the sincere welcome in her aunt's gracious, refined voice and gray eyes. How comforting she always found her aunt's company. It would be balm to her troubled heart to spend this time with her.

The hackman gave Marian a smart nod. "Thet's the lot of 'em, miss." He named the amount of the charge.

Pulling coins from her reticule, she handed them to him, including a small tip. Trying to restrain the imp within her from showing, she held a nickel out to the stranger. "Thank you for your chivalrous service, kind sir."

Dusky red raced up his neck and over his strong features. His gaze darted from the nickel in her gloved fingers to her face. Embarrassment chased away surprise, followed quickly by a look she couldn't identify, but which caused her to catch her breath in a little gasp.

"Marian, dear!"

The stranger's response all but drowned out Aunt Dorothy's mild protest. "I never accept payment for chivalrous duty, miss. Besides, you may require your funds to purchase new hair pins."

Marian dropped the nickel back into her handbag with a laugh. "*Touché.*"

Dorothy looked from one to another. "Evidently you two have met and introductions are not necessary."

"On the contrary, introductions are quite in order, Aunt Dorothy. I can't continue calling this man—as fine a man as he is —the chivalrous stranger!" It was really inexcusable, behaving in such a flirtatious manner, but the stranger had been so...proprietary, and his manner was so stiff. He couldn't be much older than twenty-five, yet somehow the term "young man" didn't fit him.

"Well, he *is* a fine man." Dorothy's pointed little chin, so like Marian's, nodded as though to settle the point. "Mr. Starr, may I introduce my niece from River's Edge, Miss Marian Ames. Marian, this is my dear friend, Mr. Everett Starr."

He acknowledged the introduction with a brisk nod and reached for a valise. "You and your niece should be getting out of this cold October rain. I'll take the trunks to Miss Ames' room while you visit."

In the pleasant parlor, Marian seated herself in one of the delicate mahogany ladies' chairs beside the fire, spreading her slim skirt to catch the benefit of the drying warmth. The room wrapped her in familiar arms. Soft light from beneath rose-colored silk brocade shades blended with the firelight to add welcome from the cold, dingy, gray afternoon outside.

Nothing had changed in the room since her last visit five years earlier. The fine old mahogany secretary still stood along one wall, regal in its stately splendor. Graceful curves of the old Beltzer love seat and matching couch, covered with deep rose raw silk, were perfect for her sweet, sophisticated aunt's parlor. The color blended well with the pale rose brocade covered chair in which she sat. Books filled a low case beside the fireplace, bound in shades of blue, brown, and russet, their leather softly worn as though well-read. It was a restful, restorative room.

"It was lovely of you to invite me, Aunt Dorothy," she greeted as her aunt sank gracefully into the grandfather's chair facing her.

"It wasn't lovely at all. It was selfish. I love having people around, and life has been altogether too quiet since Anton died five years ago, and our daughter Lucy moved East with her husband."

Guilt stabbed at Marian. "I should have visited more often."

"Nonsense, dear. You were busy with your schooling and your social life, as a young woman of nineteen should be. My maid, Sonja, has been with me for three years. She's never short on opinions and offers one of her grandmother's Swedish proverbs for every occasion. Then too, Mr. Starr and his daughter have filled a big void in this house recently."

Startled, Marian sat up a little straighter. "He *lives* here?"

"Yes, for almost a year now. Surely I've mentioned it in letters to your mother."

If so, Marian didn't recall it. She would never have accepted her aunt's hospitality if she'd suspected Dorothy of being in financial straits. A sliver of unease edged inside her chest. "I didn't realize you were taking in boarders."

"I suppose technically Mr. Starr and Aurelia are boarders, but they seem more like family. I invited them to move in after Mr. Starr's wife died last winter. Aurelia stayed with me while Mrs. Starr was ill, and we'd grown quite attached to one another. Living here allows him to keep Aurelia with him, as I or Sonja can be with the girl while he's at work."

Mr. Starr's wife was dead! No wonder he appeared to have already left youth behind. Relief shared space in her chest with sympathy. At least her suspicions of Dorothy's financial status seemed unsubstantiated. "How old is Aurelia?"

"Five." The gray eyes twinkled, and Dorothy leaned slightly forward, as though eager to talk of the girl. "She has caught my heart and caught it well."

"So little to lose a mother! Where is she now?"

"With Sonja in the kitchen. I worried at first that she would get under foot, but Sonja is from a large family, and doesn't at all mind having her about. In fact, I think she's as captured by the darling as I am. It took awhile for Aurelia to let down her guard and become friendly with Sonja, however. The little girl doesn't care for young women, as a rule."

Marian smiled. "A daddy's girl?"

A slight frown crossed Dorothy's face. "Yes, but it's more than that. I'm quite concerned about her, actually. I think it will be good for her to have you about the house."

Hurried footsteps descending the stairs interrupted her. As though by mutual consent, the women's conversation ceased, and both looked expectantly toward the parlor door which opened on the hallway.

A moment later Everett Starr appeared in the doorway. His gaze sought Marian's immediately, then drifted to where her hair still lay in waves of disarray over her shoulders, before moving quickly on to Dorothy.

Marian felt the color rise to her cheeks, warmer than the fire-heated air, in response to his notice of her hair. She brushed it behind her shoulders, trying to keep the movement discreet. It wouldn't do for him to know she'd been aware of his glance.

More disturbing was the knowledge that there had been no admiration, no hint of attraction in his gaze!

His hands were deep in the pockets of his black wool jacket, but Marian had the impression they were clenched in fists as tight as his jaw appeared clenched before he spoke. "Mrs. Dorothy, I'll take Aurelia out this evening to give you and Miss Ames time to get reacquainted. A Swedish evening is planned at the mission. Aurelia will enjoy it, and there will be plenty of food, so you needn't worry about us for dinner."

"I was so looking forward to you, Aurelia, and Marian becoming acquainted over dinner! Please reconsider." Dorothy held out an arm toward him imploringly, and he gave a small sigh before starting toward her across the thick Brussels carpet.

The "whoosh" of the pantry door was followed by the quick patter of small feet down the hallway. A tiny girl rushed into the room, pale, shoulder-length blond hair flying out behind her. A red sweater was slipping from the shoulders of her navy plaid dress.

"Papa! Papa, guess what we're havin' for dinner?"

She stopped short beside her father, wide green eyes staring at Marian. The sudden apprehension in her gaze tore at Marian's heart.

The little girl reached one hand toward her father, her fingers clutching a wad of wool trousers' leg, but her wide gaze never left Marian's face.

Mr. Starr's large hands settled gently on his daughter's thin shoulders. "Aurelia, this is Mrs. Dorothy's niece, Miss Marian Ames."

Marian wouldn't have thought the man's deep voice could be so gentle. His tenderness with his daughter was endearing.

The girl didn't acknowledge the greeting.

Marian smiled at her. "I'm pleased to meet you, Miss Aurelia. My, what lovely green eyes you have!"

Aurelia slipped both arms about her father's leg and leaned her cheek against his trouser, never ceasing to stare at Marian.

Mr. Starr slid a hand over his daughter's straight hair. "Miss Ames is staying with Mrs. Dorothy for awhile."

Aurelia looked up at him. "In *our* house?" Her voice sounded as little to Marian as a kitten's timid mew.

Mr. Starr nodded, his hand still smoothing her hair. "In Mrs. Dorothy's house, yes." He knelt beside her and grinned. "So tell me, what is it we're having for dinner?"

Aurelia looked speculatively toward Marian and didn't answer.

Her father tickled her and laughed. "Cat got your tongue, Aurelia?"

Aurelia twisted in his arms, giggling. "No. We're having roast beef, and apple pie for dessert."

"No kidding! Apple pie? Your favorite!"

She nodded.

He looked at Dorothy, who had patiently watched the entire

encounter. "I think it's best if we spent the evening here after all," he said quietly. "Give us all a chance to become comfortable with each other."

He meant it would give Aurelia a chance to be comfortable around her, Marian realized. For a moment her pride rebelled that he had wanted to leave for the evening until he thought it best for his daughter to stay. Obviously the man wasn't interested in becoming more comfortable with her, even in a friendly manner. Still, she couldn't help but admire his devotion to his child.

Aunt Dorothy had not been exaggerating when she'd said the girl was uncomfortable around young women. When she and her aunt had a minute alone, she'd ask her to explain why. The child's wide face and large green eyes certainly did catch at one's heart, as Aunt Dorothy had said.

Concerning Mr. Everett Starr, only her pride was insulted that he wasn't interested in knowing her better. After her disastrous engagement to Justin and the embarrassing fiasco which followed his marriage to Constance, she refused to become interested in another man. At least, not until she decided what she required in a man and a marriage. She was quite sure a sober widower and father would not meet her requirements.

Her gaze rested on Mr. Everett Starr's thick brown hair. His head bent over the almost white, blond hair of his daughter, and his loving, teasing murmurs came softly to her ears.

He is an especially attractive and appealing almost-young man, her heart whispered temptingly.

two

Everett rested his elbows on the wide mahogany mantle and stared at the ashes he'd just banked in the parlor fireplace. Miss Ames' golden laughter drifted down from the upstairs hallway, where she and Mrs. Dorothy were parting for the evening.

For some reason, he'd thought Mrs. Dorothy's niece would be little more than a child, in her early teen years at most. He'd never expected such a beauty; certainly not such a charming young lady with a spirit that bubbled up from within sweet and fresh as a brook in springtime.

When out on the porch he'd looked up to see her hair tumbling about her shoulders, her eyes shining, and heard her delightful laughter, Longfellow's words from *Hiawatha* had slid unbidden through his mind: "Tresses flowing like the water, and as musical a laughter; and he named her from the river, from the water-fall he named her, Minnehaha, Laughing Water."

Even now the quote left him feeling foolish. He wasn't given to spouting poetry. He couldn't recall even reading any poetry since his high school days, when Longfellow's famous poem had been required memory work. Still, the words describing the woman Hiawatha loved fit Miss Marian Ames, though the Indian woman's flowing tresses would have been far darker than this blond woman's.

In that moment when he'd first looked into her delicate face and heard her rippling laughter, his heart had let down its guard for the first time in years, and opened to her beauty and joy of life. He hadn't responded to a woman in such a manner

15

since the first months of his marriage.

A snort of a wry laugh broke from him. Some marriage his had been, some wife he'd married, some mother he'd supplied little Aurelia.

He'd not been attracted to another woman since his wife's betrayal, and he'd told himself he never cared to be. His heart had been impenetrable, and he hadn't thought to put a guard on it. There'd never been any need to do so.

Until now.

Marian Ames was nothing like his wife. That she was a lady was obvious in every movement. More than that she was...innocent. *She doesn't know anything about the grim realities of life.*

Marian was a sheltered woman. Life hadn't taught her its treacherous lessons yet, though she'd broken a few hearts and taught a few of life's unhappy lessons to a number of boys and men, or he missed his guess.

He hadn't any business at all letting his mind dwell on her. A woman like that would never have any place in his life.

He shoved the ashes about unnecessarily. It wasn't going to be easy living in the same house as the woman with the glowing eyes and infectious laugh. It wasn't going to be easy at all.

❧

"Spend the day at the mission with you?" Marian tried to hide her dismay from her aunt. "I planned to visit your dressmaker." She hesitated, seeing the hint of disappointment on Dorothy's face. "I can visit her another day. I'd love to go with you."

"Are you in need of new clothes?"

"Not truly. I have a lovely trousseau, completely unused." She gave a pretty little pout. "I don't care to wear the pieces. I've decided to put my broken engagement behind me, and start life anew. A new wardrobe always sets a woman's mind dreaming of new possibilities, don't you agree?"

Dorothy raised her hands in a gesture of amusement at the

silliness of youth and laughed. "If only life's problems were so easily left behind! However, I do agree your decision to put the past behind you and look ahead to new tomorrows is wise." Her smile died. She took Marian's hands. "I'll not push you for confidences, dear, but should you wish to discuss your engagement to Justin, I shall be here."

Marian squeezed her aunt's tiny fingers. "Thank you."

"Well, we'd best be on our way to the mission. We've only a few blocks to go, but my duty time at the nursery begins at 9:30, and it's 9:00 already."

The sunny skies belied yesterday's storm, but signs of the wind and rain in which Marian had arrived were everywhere. Small branches with green or early-turning leaves were scattered about the lawns, walks, and street. Newspapers lay in sodden, gray jumbles in puddles and against fences. Housewives covered with voluminous aprons protecting their house dresses were busy sweeping excess water and downed leaves from their front steps and walkways. Every woman they passed took time to call a greeting to Dorothy, and Dorothy returned their greetings cheerfully.

Like Dorothy's home, many of those they passed were considered elegant when built. Now they were pleasantly aging.

"Most of the people who lived here when Anton and I built our home twenty-five years ago have moved. I've come to know the Scandinavian families now living here slowly, as each moved into the area, and grown to like them as well as my original neighbors. My old friends urge me to move into a more fashionable neighborhood, but I don't care to leave the home Anton and I built, and in which we raised our children."

They turned down Second Street and the familiar odors of the nearby Mississippi River mixed with the smoke from lumber mills which took advantage of the waterways' famous Falls of St. Anthony for power. Large rectangular stacks of delightfully resin-scented pine covered numerous lots. Like River's

Edge, Minneapolis was a lumber town. Marian found the familiarity surprisingly comforting.

"Many of the men whose families use the mission's services work in the lumber and flour mills along the river," Dorothy informed her. "They live in this neighborhood, the west bank of the river, south of the business district. The people are primarily first- or second-generation immigrants. We try to assist them in learning the ways and language of America, and care for their children while they work. The mission is now called the Plymouth Kindergarten and Industrial Association, but citizens still refer to it as the mission."

Between Thirteenth and Fourteenth Avenues South, Dorothy announced brightly, "Here we are!" A fine, large, clapboard, three-story building with freshly painted cream-colored walls and leaf-green trim stood before them. Its roof peaked in high gables with a round open tower rising in the midst of them. On the opposite side of the house, a fenced playground was in view, though empty of children at the moment.

The front door entered into a wide hallway painted a pale ivory above oak wainscoting. A woman with a long, sharp nose and black hair streaked with gray, worn in a neat but simple bun, was seated at a ladies' desk near the door. Dorothy introduced her as Mrs. Turner. Marian was taken aback at the cold, direct look in her dark eyes.

Mrs. Turner agreed to show Marian about while Dorothy reported to the nursery. Marian repressed a giggle while following the woman's straight-as-a-pin back down the hallway. How had this woman been selected to be a greeter? Perhaps the people in charge hoped she would scare away people who didn't need the organization's services!

Numerous doors opened off both sides of the hallway, and Mrs. Turner informed her the day nursery was on one side, the free kindergarten on the other. Placing an index finger primly over her rigid lips to indicate silence, she opened a door.

White iron cribs lined one wall of the cheerful room, tasteful paintings of Mary and the baby Jesus hanging above them. Comfortable wicker rockers with high backs and wide, round arms invited the workers to rest with their charges. The cribs were filled with babes, and youngsters played contentedly about the room under the watchful eyes of Dorothy and three other women.

Mrs. Turner closed the door quietly. "We care for over three dozen children daily in the nursery. Mothers begin bringing them in around six."

"Six in the morning?" Marian was appalled. She was seldom out of bed by that time.

Mrs. Turner pinned her with an indignant look. "Naturally in the morning. The mothers leave them on their way to their positions. Most of the mothers work as domestics or for tailors. They retrieve their children on their way home, often as late as seven." She gave Marian a cold stare. "That is seven in the evening."

Marian swallowed a chuckle and followed her up the wide wooden staircase at the end of the hall. On one side of the large hall a room ran the length of the house, front to back. Large rectangular oak tables surrounded by strictly functional chairs filled the room. A generous number of lights hung from the ceiling. Shelves along the walls held bolts of fabric, catalogs, spools of thread, and envelopes of needles.

Marian grinned at Mrs. Turner. "You needn't explain the use of this room. Sewing classes must be held here."

Mrs. Turner didn't return her smile. "One hundred teen-age girls take the courses. They are encouraged with prizes for punctuality, attendance, and cleanliness in addition to performance and improvement. The sewing classes are held in the afternoons, and on Tuesday evenings. Other evenings this hall and the one opposite are used for mothers' meetings, where mothers can learn of Froebelian methods, what is being taught their children in kindergarten and why, and ways in which they can help their children learn properly at home. There are also industrial classes on managing an efficient household on a modest budget. Monday evenings, Mr. Starr leads English classes."

The name jolted Marian to attention. "Mr. Everett Starr?" Aunt Dorothy hadn't told her he worked at the mission.

She wouldn't have thought Mrs. Turner's thin lips could be compressed any tighter. "Precisely."

Proceeding back downstairs, Mrs. Turner listed some of the mission's other efforts with a tone which implied she had repeated the list scores of times. "The Kitchen Garden Club gives classes in cooking, sewing, deportment, bed making, care of a kitchen broom, and so forth. It is hoped some of their lessons will take root and be used to improve their present homes and those of the future. Then, of course, we hope the young women will see that being a domestic can be as much a way of serving God as more glorified ministries." She sighed eloquently. "The servant problem never has been adequately solved."

Marian wondered whether it was for God's benefit or her own that Mrs. Turner wished domestics to see their work as heaven-ordered.

"We have two permanent female staff who live at the house. Their rooms are on the third floor and offer them much needed privacy at the end of the day."

Marian could well imagine the privacy was much needed! What extraordinary women they must be to live in such a public building!

"In the basement we have the kitchen facilities and cafeteria, for naturally we must feed the kindergarten and day nursery children. In the building next door classes are held for boys. If you would like to view it, I can show it to you." Mrs. Turner's tone indicated she hoped Marian would say no.

Instead Marian gave her a gracious smile. "I should love to

see everything your church is doing here. It's very kind of you to take the time to show me about."

"It's my duty," was the terse reply.

When they neared the building, Mrs. Turner informed her Everett was in charge of the classes. "One would think the church could find a more suitable man for a position which influences the city's youths' morals. Any man who would tolerate his wife's immoral actions, as Mr. Starr did, cannot have a shred of decency."

Disapproval surrounded her like smoke from the mills smokestacks surrounded the neighborhood on a still day. Marian had no idea what the woman considered "his wife's immoral actions," but she knew Aunt Dorothy would never allow any but an honorable man to live under her roof.

They entered by the back door, passed through a small cloakroom, and entered a large room that filled the rest of the first floor.

The walls were covered with wooden pegs from which hung men's work aprons and saws, planes and mallets. Vices for woodwork gripped some of the workbenches. Near the ceiling hung fine old prints and etchings of men busy at different crafts.

"The woodworking shop," Mrs. Turner explained succinctly.

Marian barely heard the unnecessary words. Her gaze was caught in the surprised gaze of Mr. Starr. The intensity in the deep-set brown eyes caused her heart to clench in a most unfamiliar manner.

In his denim shirt, he appeared much more the workingman than he had when they'd met and she'd teased him about acting a hackman's helper.

He laid down a nail and mallet and started toward them, wiping his hands along the coarse workman's apron covering his brown corduroy trousers.

"This is Miss Marian Ames, Mrs. Dorothy Lindstrom's niece. I'm showing her about the mission."

Mr. Starr nodded. "We've met. I'll show her the workrooms. I'm sure you need to return to your post."

Mrs. Turner's already thin lips pressed into an even thinner line, and she darted a suspicious glance from him to Marian and back again. "I suppose that will be acceptable."

She didn't move to leave.

Mr. Starr's hands settled on his hips. "Perhaps Miss Ames has seen enough of the workshop and would like to return with you."

Marian clasped her hands behind her and smiled brightly. "On the contrary; I'm all a-tremble with excitement to see where the industrial arts are taught."

Mrs. Turner looked pointedly at the small gold watch pinned to her blouse. "I shouldn't think it would take too long. I'll look for your return in no more than fifteen minutes."

Without further ado, she marched through the swinging door into the entryway. A moment later they heard the back door slam.

Marian could hold back no longer; her soft laughter filled the room. She leaned ever so slightly toward Everett, her hands still caught lightly behind her back. "Isn't she incredible? One would think the country could use her in military training."

She delighted in his unexpected shout of laughter. She'd begun to think the somber man incapable of the happy sound.

"She can appear rather fierce, can't she?" he agreed. "But she's been a faithful worker at the mission since it was started."

"Next time I find myself thinking what a sourpuss face she has, I'll call that favorable fact to mind."

She caught the admiration in the eyes whose gaze rested on her face before sliding quickly over her gown.

When his glance returned to her face, the friendliness was gone, replaced with a polite but emotionless façade that made her feel ridiculously as though she'd been judged and found lacking. Hadn't he cared for her fashionable emerald green gown?

Quite casually he retreated until a worn workbench stood between them. "Have you ever been in a wood workshop?"

"No, though I do have an idea how some of the tools are used—mallets and saws and nails, for instance." She grinned across at him.

He nodded toward the wall behind her. "Some of the students' work is displayed there."

Small tables and chests stood on the floor in all stages of development. Wooden boxes of various sizes lined the shelves, some starkly simple, others carved with fascinating designs. Cornices mixed with the boxes, creating an interesting effect.

She ran a hand lightly over one of the more intricately carved boxes. Its highly glossed surface was smoother than ice. "I'm impressed with the quality of the work. Are any of these pieces yours?"

He didn't answer at first, and she looked at him questioningly, still holding the box. He swallowed, his Adam's apple jerking, and she wondered what she'd said to upset him.

"The box you're holding is one of mine."

She gave a little gasp of pleasure. "Truly? It's most beautiful! You're a fine artist."

He looked away. She noticed his lips compress tightly and his hands dig into his back pockets. Was he upset with her for handling the box? She set it back carefully.

"What were you working on when we entered?"

She followed him to the table where she'd first seen him. "I'm repairing one of the kindergarten chairs." He shook his head, clasped one of the columns of turned wood in the back of the little oak chair, and almost smiled. "Can't imagine how those tykes managed to break the leg on it."

"The child obviously didn't know his own strength."

The chuckle she'd hoped to gain from him never came.

"Do you spend much of your time making repairs for the mission?"

"When necessary, I make repairs during the day. Most classes

are held in the evenings, when the boys can get away from
school or work to attend."

"Both boys and men attend?"

His face looked suddenly harsh, and the knuckles of the hand
still clasping the wooden pole on the chair whitened. "Yes.
Too many boys and young men are pushed into the hard and
unrewarding life of industry, where they work long hours at
hard labor in dark, improperly vented rooms. My hope is some
of the newsboys and shoeblacks and delivery boys can learn
skills here that will help them obtain more enjoyable and health-
ful positions."

"Rather like a trade school?"

"Not especially. This is the first year the mission has had a
woodworking shop, so we teach primarily basic woodworking.
We've plans for improvement, however. In addition to general
woodworking, we do teach *sloyd*."

"What is that?"

"A Swedish form of woodcrafting. Lars Erickson introduced
it to America in 'eighty-four, here in Minneapolis, and became
the church's first instructor. That's where I learned it. He's
living in Boston now, where *sloyd* is receiving enthusiastic
acceptance. It's more highly skilled than general woodworking."

"It sounds a wonderful opportunity for immigrant boys."

"Nearly all the woodcarvers in the city are Scandinavian-
born. Most youngsters aren't interested in learning a skill they
can't put to work in a mill or factory. Too much time to learn
and too little return for their money."

"You mean, they wish to train for more profitable careers."

"If that's how you term the positions provided by the indus-
trialists."

Marian frowned. "I thought industry was good for the working people. It supplies jobs, after all."

He gave a sharp imitation of a laugh. "Industry is beneficial, all right, if you don't happen to work for a company that sees its employees as nothing more than work mules."

"Your attitude is rather harsh." This obviously wasn't the proper time to tell him that her father owned a sawmill in River's Edge.

He withdrew further behind his already cool expression. "Do you ever read the labor union articles in the newspaper, Miss Ames?"

"I've never seen any such articles in the River's Edge paper, although we do have a large lumber industry." And her father spoke often and loudly against unions, she added silently.

"The *Minneapolis Tribune* carries such articles each Sunday. I recommend you read them."

The condescension in his tone poured anger through her.

"I shall, and then perhaps we can have this discussion again, after I've broadened my horizons." She didn't try to keep the sarcasm from her voice. Turning on her heel, she started across the room. "I'd best get back to the other building, before Mrs. Turner comes looking for me."

⁊ⱥ

Everett threw his mallet down in disgust and rubbed the back of his neck wearily. The muscles felt like metal rods. He walked toward the window that looked out on the mission building next door. He couldn't concentrate on his work a whit since walking Marian back there. The flower-like fragrance she wore still hung in the air, teasing at his senses. He wouldn't have thought such a light scent could hold its own against the heavy smells of pine sawdust, acids, enamels, and metal.

He hadn't been able to put Miss Marian Ames out his thoughts for a single waking hour since he'd met her. Now that she'd physically invaded his work space, it would be more difficult than ever to do so.

Her appreciation of his artistry with the carved box had thrilled him, then squeezed his heart painfully. His wife had never realized there was any artistry involved with his work. She'd ridiculed his vocation ceaselessly, openly belittling his efforts. Her remarks lived on after her to plague him, no matter how many others praised his works.

No one else's compliments had affected him like Marian's.

Her comments about industry and the laboring man had made it plainer than ever that he and Marian were from different worlds. He'd angered her with his comments. She'd realized he was insinuating she was innocent and ignorant of the real world.

Well, she was. Perhaps it was best she was angry. It certainly wasn't doing his heart any good having her smiling sweetly at him as she'd done when she'd first entered this room. Before he could catch himself, he'd been laughing with her. It had taken him a few minutes and a difficult struggle with himself to build a barrier between them again.

She'd caught him off guard, that was all, coming into his shop unexpectedly. A smile stretched his lips, and the view out the window faded. The same way she'd surprised him with her wonderful eyes and laughter when he'd looked into her face for the first time on the porch yesterday, and seen her loveliness amidst that marvelous tumble of hair. *By Henry, but she was beautiful!*

He started resolutely toward the workbench. He'd have to keep his guard up from now on. It wouldn't do to let himself fall for Marian Ames with her innocence and sophisticated loveliness. A woman like that wasn't meant for him. Falling for her would only mean having his heart scraped raw a second time. There was no way he was going to put himself through that again.

three

Marian entered the mission's front door without a backward glance at Everett Starr. He'd accompanied her from next door in silence, in spite of her protest that his presence was unnecessary for such a short walk.

Her chin rose half an inch. The man had as much as said she was too ignorant of the business world to have an opinion on labor matters. Well, she certainly had sense enough to realize that with the extremely high unemployment in this year of 1893, a person had no reason to complain if he had a position, regardless of the conditions or amount of pay.

Mrs. Turner glanced at her suspiciously and informed her Dorothy was in the kindergarten room. Marian thanked her and opened the wide door she indicated.

The room was wide and spacious, with oak wainscoting five feet high beneath robin's-egg blue walls. Portraits of Abraham Lincoln and George Washington mixed with small flags to decorate the walls.

The children were seated in groups of a dozen at low, rectangular tables in chairs like the one Mr. Starr was repairing. Children's voices filled the room with a high-pitched buzz, though the youngsters were orderly and their talking was kept at moderate levels. There were over fifty children in the room, with only two young women and Aunt Dorothy moving among them for supervision.

Walking between the tables to reach Aunt Dorothy, Marian noticed the children playing with brightly colored wooden blocks at one table, and drawing pictures with thick pencils at another. The children seemed eager in their pursuits, reaching to try another's toy, or to show a supervisor his work. In one corner sat a large box of sand, empty of children at the moment. The slate along one wall was filled with chalk drawings of stick people. A dark upright piano stood beside it.

"I feel I must stay for the day's duration," Dorothy explained when Marian asked her plans. "There are so many supervisors out ill that both the kindergarten and nursery are understaffed. If you would like to return to the house, I'm sure Mr. Starr will escort you."

As though she would ask him! "That won't be necessary. I'll be glad to stay as long as you need. Perhaps I can be of assistance."

Aunt Dorothy's shining eyes rewarded her offer, and Marian hoped her aunt wouldn't realize how reluctantly it was made. She'd never supervised more than a few children at once. She had serious doubts as to her ability in this situation.

Aunt Dorothy quickly introduced her to the young woman in charge of the room, Miss Jessie Watkins, and it was decided Dorothy would return to the nursery while Marian helped with the kindergarten. Marian was sorely tempted to follow quickly on Dorothy's heels when she left. If anyone had told her a week ago that a group of four- and five-year-olds would leave her panicked, she would have laughed heartily. She wasn't laughing now.

"I. . .I'm not certain what to do," she admitted to Miss Watkins, a woman with mousy brown hair worn on top of her head, plain features, an unpretentious manner, and the kindest eyes Marian had ever seen.

"It's almost story-time. My assistants usually prepare the children's snack during this time. If you read the story, it will help immeasurably. Then I can prepare the room for the next activity."

Marian agreed, and Miss Watkins brought her a book of children's stories, recommending *The Lion and the Mouse*, and Marian refamiliarized herself with the popular story.

It went far better than she'd anticipated. Fortunately she knew the story well enough to tell it without reading it and so could look into the children's faces when she spoke. By the time she was a few lines into the story, she'd forgotten herself in the joy of making the story come alive for the children. They sat on the floor, leaning toward her eagerly, their eyes never leaving her face.

In the midst of the story, her gaze met Aurelia's, and she stumbled in the middle of a sentence. She hadn't realized the girl would be in the class. Aurelia's attention was caught by the story, but she wasn't deeply involved like most of the children. Even here she seemed self-conscious and withdrawn for a little one, and Marian's heart went out to her.

Grins of satisfaction filled the children's faces at the Lion's last line in the story: "Little friends are great friends."

After the snack, the children were allowed outside to use the playground. Marian was flattered at the number of children, little girls especially, who flocked about her. They wanted to tell her all about themselves, and to touch her soft green gown. But Aurelia wasn't among them.

At least Aurelia hadn't retreated to a corner of the ground to play alone, Marian thought, watching the girl tossing a large rubber ball with half-a-dozen others.

Between noon and one o'clock mothers, brothers, and sisters stopped for the children. It seemed to Marian that just as many children remained, their parents and siblings working and unable to collect the children until evening. The kindergarten room turned into a babysitting service, with organized play and nap time.

The most emotional part of the day for Marian was when mothers began picking up their children that evening. Many of them did not arrive until after dark. They came in simple clothing, often covered with worn jackets and large shawls or scarves. Their faces looked tired and drawn, but most greeted their children and the supervisors with smiles. A large number had their arms full of clothing.

The women's gazes slid over Marian as impersonally as though she were a dress form in a window display, noting the elegance of her costly day dress. Though the women returned Marian's greetings, their faces were closed to her. Marian wished she could believe it was because she was a stranger, but she knew it was in most part because her gown set her in a different social class.

Aurelia was the last child left. She sat on the piano stool, patiently playing her own no-melody tunes with a pudgy index finger. Jessie said Aurelia often waited for Dorothy or her father to finish their work.

She shook her head sadly. "Most of the children this age become attached to their teachers quickly. Aurelia still keeps me at arms' length. Trusting is difficult for her, of course, after her experience with her mother."

"You mean with her mother's death?"

Jessie glanced at her sharply. "Partly," she answered cautiously.

"I don't understand."

"Being Dorothy's niece and staying under the same roof with Mr. Starr and Aurelia, I thought you knew Mr. and Mrs. Starr's story. It's not my place to share it. Forgive me for raising the subject."

She broke off abruptly, returning to restoring order to the room, leaving Marian frustrated and confused. Why did people keep hinting at something unusual about Everett's marriage? What had happened to hurt Aurelia so deeply?

She had no choice at the moment but to abandon the topic.

Helping Jessie place the chairs on the tables to clear the area for sweeping, Marian asked about the piles of clothing so many mothers carried.

"The women are seamstresses. They are paid by the piece rather than by the hour. They work on pieces at home in the evening in order to complete them sooner, and thereby increase their income."

"But the women have already put in a full day's work, and have their families and homes to care for in the evenings."

"Yes. Many work twelve-hour days before picking up their children. However, times are hard. With the economic depression, many of the women's husbands and boys are out of work. Their income is needed now more than ever."

Marian set down a small chair and stared at Jessie, confused. How could the woman who spent long days caring for these women's children be so unaffected by their home conditions? "You seem very accepting of the fact of their overwork."

Jessie looked at her squarely and explained quietly. "I try to see things as they truly are, and then do what I can to help. Knowing that while they work their children are safe and happy with us, and that none of the family's hard-earned dollars are paying for their children's care, is a great aid to them. I'm trained to teach, with special training in teaching kindergarten. Therefore, the best way I can use my time and skill to help these mothers is by doing exactly what I am doing."

"Of course." Marian rubbed her palms lightly over the fabric covering her hips. "Forgive me for sounding so foolishly judgmental. I've never been closely associated with. . ." She struggled to find a term to replace the one on the tip of her tongue: working people. She wasn't successful.

Jessie went back to moving chairs, and Marian joined her. "Will you be helping at the mission while you're visiting your aunt, Marian?"

After spending the day here and seeing the great need, Marian knew she wanted to be part of it. "I'd like to help, but I have no training."

"The Kitchen and Garden Club would rejoice to have your assistance, I'm sure. The members are responsible for the sewing, cooking, housekeeping, and deportment classes for older girls."

Marian wrinkled her nose. "Deportment is the only area in

which I have knowledge. I've never sewn or cooked. I've planned menus often, but never on a budget." She decided it was best not to mention furnishing the huge home for her wealthy former fiancé in anticipation of their marriage. The amount of Justin's money she'd spent on the house would have healthily supported this mission for years. The thought made her slightly sick to her stomach.

Jessie smiled. "No one can be good at everything. The Kitchen and Garden Club is happiest when I'm too busy with the children to help with the Club, if the truth be known. You're very good with children, though."

"I've always gotten on well with children. Still, I don't know how much help I could be even in the nursery. I've never changed a diaper or given a baby a bath."

"You're a natural-born storyteller. The children were on the edge of their seats, figuratively speaking. They loved the deep voice you gave the lion and the high, squeaky voice you gave the mouse."

"You're very gracious, Jessie, but I can't spend the day telling stories."

"I'd be glad for your assistance in the kindergarten. The children flock to you, and rapport with them is the most important thing. I can explain to you what activities we'll be doing each day, and the reason for them, if you're interested in learning."

"I'd like that!"

"I've a number of books on kindergarten and teaching. I'll lend you some. I teach a kindergarten-instructor training course here at the mission on Tuesday evenings. If after a few days with us you're still interested, you may wish to join the class."

So she was to be given a probationary period. Well, it was probably best. "Thank you, Jessie."

It was almost seven-thirty when Dorothy, Marian, Mr. Starr, and Aurelia arrived home. Sonja, the live-in maid and cook, complained numerous times over the dried-out roast. The four from the mission were too tired and hungry to be upset at the overcooked meal.

After dinner Marian perused her wardrobe. She hadn't anything suitable to wear to the mission; nothing that wouldn't offend the working mothers, that is. Her trousseau had been selected with her fiancé's position in mind. As wife of one of the wealthiest businessmen in southeastern Minnesota, she would have been expected to dress accordingly.

She would simply have to spend tomorrow shopping. She'd warned Jessie she wouldn't be returning for two days, so she had the day free.

Her decision made, she went downstairs to tell Dorothy her plan. Her entrance to the parlor was greeted by a loud "Shhh!"

She stopped short, then saw the silencer was Aurelia. The little girl was sitting on her father's lap in an overstuffed chair in a corner beneath a rose silk-and-tassel covered lamp. The lamp and the dying flames in the fireplace were the only light in the room.

"Papa's sleeping," Aurelia informed her in a moderate whisper.

Indeed he was. Marian smiled. One of his arms still encircled Aurelia, but his head had slid to one side, revealing the crocheted tidy on the chair's back. His chin rested on his chest and his breath came evenly. Aurelia held a book of nursery stories he had evidently been reading before falling asleep.

The sight tugged at Marian's heart. *What a homey family scene!*

She tiptoed nearer to whisper to Aurelia, "Would you like me to read to you for a bit?"

The little girl barely shook her head. "If I move, Papa might wake up. He needs his sleep. He's awful tired."

A door slammed in another part of the house, and he stirred. A moment later his shoulders shifted. He stretched his neck, his eyes still closed. When he opened them, he was looking right into Marian's eyes.

She grinned. "Hi, sleepyhead."

He sat up straighter, his arm tightening around Aurelia. His gaze shifted to the girl and softened. "Did I fall asleep before finishing the story again?"

Aurelia tucked her chin and looked up at him with a silly smile. "Yes, Papa."

His free hand slipped behind her neck and he touched her forehead with a kiss. "Sorry, sweetheart. I'll try to do better tomorrow night."

"It's all right, Papa. I know how the story ends anyway."

Marian walked to the fireplace, picking up the poker to stir the dying embers. She felt as though she'd unintentionally intruded on a private part of their lives. Still, she was glad for the moment. It had given her a peek at the heart of the sober, strong man. She liked what she'd seen. She'd seldom observed such tenderness in a man.

He sent Aurelia from the room with instructions to wash and change for bed. The child's footsteps barely died away before he was standing beside her at the fireplace. After the touching scene she'd just witnessed, his nearness was especially unsettling. She continued unnecessarily to poke at the embers.

"Did you enjoy your day at the mission, Miss Ames?"

"It was interesting. When Aunt Dorothy spoke of the mission I had no idea that so many services are performed there. It's not like charity work. It's more a becoming one with the community, part of the people's lives, living Christ's love with each other."

"Yes, that's what the church intends. Not many understand the distinction."

She was absurdly flattered by his approving tone.

"It reminds me of Hull House, the settlement house in Chicago."

"There are many similarities. It's been said a settlement is 'a kindergarten for adults,' and that Mother's Meetings are a settlement's most important work. The mission started the first free kindergarten in the city, back in 1880."

"My goodness, it certainly predates Hull House then, doesn't it?"

The silence grew long between them, and the sound of the embers popping was loud in the quiet room. Marian couldn't think of a thing to say, which was an unusual state for her.

She almost jumped when he finally spoke. "Is something distressing you? You appear exceptionally subdued this evening."

She set the poker back on its wrought-iron rack and rubbed her palms lightly together, avoiding his eyes. "Jessie Watkins, the kindergarten teacher, asked whether I'd help at the mission. I said yes."

She glanced up at him. Surprise stopped her thoughts at the light shining in his eyes, and it was a moment before she could recollect them to continue. "I have never felt as worthless as I did today."

He leaned an elbow on the wide mahogany mantle and his brows met. "Worthless?"

She spread her hands wide, palms upward. "I have so little to offer." Uncomfortable, she began pacing. "I've had the traditional young society woman's education. I can tell you all about famous literature and well-known paintings and sculptures."

She turned about with a little laugh to face him again. "I can repeat the proper use of calling cards, and how often one should visit another member of society, and at what time of day, and how long one should stay. Should you plan a dinner party, I can write a lovely invitation, plan a wonderful menu, choose a fashionable gown certain to be commented on in the society columns—I'm especially good at that—seat everyone in the proper place, and carry on delightful dinner conversation. However, beyond fancy needlework, I can't sew or cook or do anything else useful at the mission."

She wanted to pull her gaze from his, but couldn't. His eyes were compelling, though she couldn't decipher the emotions behind them. That in itself was unsettling.

"But you told Jessie you'd return?"

She nodded.

"Tomorrow?"

"No. Not tomorrow."

His gaze dropped to the thick carpet. "I see."

What did he see? Why did he sound disappointed?

"There are certain items I must purchase. I'll be going shopping tomorrow. I intend to return to the mission the following day."

He only nodded.

She hated his quiet. Did he think she didn't truly intend to return to the mission? For some reason she didn't understand and certainly wasn't ready to analyze, it was important to her to have his respect. "Is there anything I can purchase for you while I'm out? That is, anything you would like me to purchase for Aurelia?"

His lips twisted in a mockery of a smile. "I doubt you'll be shopping at a place my pocketbook can afford."

Her shoulders settled back slightly. "I assure you I'll be stopping at common stores. If you doubt my ability to select items for your daughter—" She shrugged.

"I didn't mean to insult you."

"I believe you meant to do exactly that."

Consternation darted through his eyes. "You're right. Please forgive me. You've done nothing to elicit such a comment." He rubbed his hand over his chin. "The truth is, Aurelia needs some clothes, and I haven't the slightest idea what to purchase. I usually get clothing for her from the donations at the mission, and they seldom fit properly. It's not that I can't afford to buy new clothing for her. I guess going to the stores when I don't know what I'm looking for is uncomfortable, and the mission donations are convenient." He grimaced. "It's rotten unfair to Aurelia."

She couldn't contain a smile. "Yes, it is."

He looked away, struggled with a smile of his own, and lost. "Couldn't stop yourself from agreeing, could you? You are a most direct young woman."

Her smile broadened. "What would you like me to purchase, and how much would you like me to spend?"

He dug out his pocketbook and handed her twenty dollars. "She needs everything from the skin out. Do you think that will cover it?"

It certainly wouldn't have "covered it" at the type of stores at which she was accustomed to shopping. She had no idea if it would "cover it" at the emporiums she'd be stopping at tomorrow. "I'll try to keep the purchases within this."

"I can afford more if necessary."

Sonja entered the room to give it a final straightening for the day, humming a tune softly. Everett and Marian glanced at her casually, continuing their conversation.

"Do you think Aurelia might accompany me?"

He didn't try to sweeten his answer. "I don't know. I'll try to convince her it's best and that she'll be fine with you, but if she adamantly refuses, we'd best put the idea off." He rubbed his hand over the back of his neck, and sympathy for him warmed her chest at the weary look that crossed his face. "I guess you've noticed she doesn't trust young women much."

"Perhaps that's not so strange after losing her mother. Her love for you is obvious."

The sound of tiny feet hurrying down the hallway ended their conversation. A moment later Aurelia hurried in to throw her arms about her father and urge him to tuck her into bed.

While Marian watched them leave, Sonja stopped beside her, checking to see that the fire was safely banked. She sighed deeply. "*'Bränt barn skyr elden.'*"

"Excuse me?"

The maid flushed. "Vun of *Mormor*'s Svedish proverbs—I

mean, my grandmother's proverbs."

"What does it mean?"

"'A burnt child shuns the fire.'"

"Are you saying Aurelia believes all young women will die and leave her like her mother did?"

The wide eyes flashed with surprise. "Oh, no, miss! She's afraid they vill dislike her und send her avay, as her mother did." Sonja fingered her apron nervously. "It's not my place to speak of such tings. Good night, miss."

Marian was too stunned at Sonja's revelation to urge her to stay. Had Aurelia's mother truly sent the girl away? Surely Everett would never have allowed it. Aurelia was obviously his entire world.

But Mrs. Turner, too, had indicated that something unworthy or sinister lurked in Everett's past, something to do with his marriage. One couldn't see Everett with Aurelia and doubt his character, she assured herself, pulling the cord to the corner lamp.

Aunt Dorothy had said Aurelia lived with her during Mrs. Starr's last illness. Possibly the child misunderstood the circumstances. Sonja's tale was likely the end result of a train of gossip.

She'd come to Minneapolis to start over. She'd told God she wanted to live for Him instead of herself. Well, her life certainly had changed considerably within thirty-six hours and a sixty-mile trip up the Mississippi River. Working at a settlement-style mission, planning to purchase nondescript clothing, and living in the same house as a timid, withdrawn child and her sober, somewhat bitter father, however, wasn't the change she'd expected.

Does God always work like that, turning people's lives topsy-turvy? Well, it would be interesting to see what He does next!

four

I can hardly believe Aurelia agreed to accompany me, Marian thought as they passed from Olson's large emporium into the bright sunshine of Nicollet Avenue.

When Aurelia had said yes, her father's face had split with a grin. The joy in his gaze when it met hers over the child's head had melted her heart. What was it about a man showing his love for a child that was so endearing?

Numerous times during the shopping trip Marian was sorely tempted to go against her promise to Everett and take Aurelia to one of the best establishments. It would be such fun to purchase even one choice frock for the girl, but it wouldn't be fair to her father to do so. After spending yesterday at the mission, honesty made her admit such a frock would have no place in Aurelia's life.

She was somewhat ashamed of her own reaction to purchasing her simple gowns for wear at the mission. Even though she selected the best ready-made day dresses the Emporium had to offer, the items were cheap compared to the clothing to which she was accustomed.

Their arms filled with Aurelia's purchases, they walked down Nicollet Avenue, Minneapolis' busiest street. Marian had to take care not to step on her skirt, and envied Aurelia her mid-calf length dress. The constant clang of the electric green and yellow trolley cars mixed with the whinnies and clopping of horses pulling carriages, wagons, cabs, and covered delivery conveyances. Three-story brick and stone buildings each side of the street gave the feeling of walking through a canyon.

The walks were filled with women shoppers dressed in

everything from the latest hats and day gowns to simple, worn skirts and shawls. Newsboys, shoeblacks, and deliverymen moved among them, an occasional clerk or business man in a suit and derby standing out from the crowd.

The two had barely turned onto Washington Avenue when they came to an abrupt halt. The sidewalk was filled with newsboys gathered in a jabbering group, each with a large sheet in one hand, and newspapers beneath one arm.

Aurelia shouted joyfully, "Papa!"

A moment later the little girl started headlong into the fray of boys, trying with only a modicum of success to edge them aside with her elbows and packages.

"Aurelia, stop!" Frustration filled Marian. Her hands were so full of packages she couldn't physically stop the girl. *Why in the world would she think her father would be here, in the midst of these dirty, ragged boys, instead of at the mission?*

"Aurelia!"

At the sound of Everett's deep voice, Marian's gaze moved from trying to follow the girl's back through the throng to search for him. She found him in a moment, in the very midst of the boys.

Everett's voice had an effect on the boys, too. They moved from Aurelia's way to make a path for her to her father. She was beside him in an instant, her face as happy as a sunbeam. "Papa, wait 'til you see what I bought!"

The boys' attention was no longer on the papers they held. A number of them were looking Marian over with glances that made her want to melt into the paved street to get away. In spite of her discomfort, she couldn't help but be shocked that such lecherous looks were coming from such young boys. Hadn't anyone cared enough to raise them properly?

One of the tallest boys, his long straight hair falling over his eyebrows in front and frayed jacket collar in back, tossed out, "These yer kid and old lady, Mr. Starr?"

Everett's palm bumped the back of the boy's bicycle hat with just enough force to knock it over the boy's eyes. "A gentleman never refers to a woman as an 'old lady,' Jules."

Marian was glad the anger in his voice wasn't directed at her!

A short, fat boy beside Jules grinned up at Everett. "What if the woman *is* old?"

"Then you're especially careful not to call her an old lady." Everett winked at the boy. The troupe guffawed.

Everett's hands rested on Aurelia's shoulders and she leaned against his trousers. "This is my daughter, Aurelia. The young woman is Miss Ames, and no, she is not my wife."

"Are you goin' to marry her or somepin'?"

Marian didn't see who asked the question that spread warm color over her face.

"Miss Ames and I are only friends. Now why don't all of you head into the next block and see if you can identify the next place on the list. I'll catch up to you in a minute."

The group immediately started in the direction from which Marian and Aurelia had come, parting to go around her like the nearby Mississippi River around an island. She tried to ignore the insolent looks some of them continued to give her, but they were discomforting.

She found it harder to ignore Jules' last comment to Everett before he followed the rest of the boys. "If I were you, Mr. Starr, I think I'd try ta make that friendship a bit more personal."

She knew her cheeks were still flushed when the three of them were finally left alone, and she hoped Everett would think the color was from the autumn wind shooting briskly through the downtown streets, captured by the many high buildings.

"I'm sorry if they insulted you." His steady gaze was troubled. "They haven't much training in manners, I'm afraid. What they've had, they try to forget. Manners don't impress the other boys on the street much."

She didn't want to admit the uneasiness she'd felt in the boys' presence. "I didn't expect to see you here."

He grinned. "In spite of the fact that I knew you were shopping today, I didn't expect to run across you on *Snus* Boulevard either."

Marian frowned. "*Snus* Boulevard? I thought this was Washington Avenue."

"That's the formal name. It's more popularly known as *Snus* Boulevard because of all the tobacco-chewing Scandinavians that have their businesses on the avenue."

"Oh. I was surprised to see how many shops appear abandoned."

He nodded. "Entire blocks of businesses are closed in some cases, due to the depression. The economic conditions don't help those boys you saw any."

"Are they from the mission?"

"Not exactly. The church has a Newsboys' Club that meets on Sunday mornings for Sunday School, followed by a warm meal for the boys, but it isn't held at the mission. A lot of the boys don't get many warm meals. We've started a banking system for them, too. Most of the boys try to give ten percent of their earnings to the church each week, and bank at least a little of their earnings. Not easy for them with the depression on. Those living with their families share their earnings with them, and as little as that is, it's needed more than ever when the fathers are out of work."

"This wasn't a Sunday school class today, surely?"

"No, it's a map-reading course. They've been begging me to give them one, even though a number of them can barely read."

"Papa," Aurelia interrupted with a determined tug on his trousers. "I want to tell you what I bought."

In a swift movement, she was in his arms, packages and all. Marian thought enviously that when the two of them smiled at each other, they entered a world of their own.

"I'm eager to hear what you bought, sweetheart, but I need to go with the boys. Your new things are going to look beautiful on you, though, I just know it. Can't wait to see you in them. Will you try them on for me after dinner?"

Aurelia nodded, disappointment in every sag of her body.

Everett pressed his cheek to hers and set her down. "I'll look forward to it all day."

His promise brought a pleased smile to Aurelia's wide face. His steady gaze met Marian's. "Thank you for taking her with you. Better take the trolley as much of the way home as possible. Washington Avenue passes through some rather rough areas."

He was gone a moment later, and Aurelia's attitude slipped immediately back into one of a polite but detached companion. Her lack of friendliness twisted at Marian's chest. Her pain wasn't for herself but for Aurelia. The child needed the warmth of friendship, needed to be able to care for someone other than her father and Aunt Dorothy. She wished she knew how to help the girl.

In an attempt to cheer her, Marian stopped at a soda fountain and treated her to a sundae. Aurelia seemed to enjoy the sweet, but it didn't make her actions toward Marian any warmer.

Marian was surprised that evening, therefore, when Aurelia went into detail in describing the shop and sundae to her father, her face animated and alight with excitement at the memory.

The child could barely contain herself until dinner was over and she could finally show her purchases to her father. On Aurelia's orders, Everett and Aunt Dorothy waited in the parlor while she changed into her new outfits. She grudgingly allowed Marian to help her dress, since Marian had already seen the new clothes. But when the first new dress was securely fastened and Marian held out her hand to the girl to walk together to the parlor, Aurelia ignored her and ran down the hall alone, leaving Marian to follow.

Everett and Dorothy were appropriately appreciative of Aurelia's first outfit, and the girl fairly beamed her pleasure. She turned carefully for them, holding out the fabric striped alternately in pale and dark blue. The huge white cape collar was trimmed with tiny lace. A navy velvet ribbon went around the dress just below the collar and ended in a large bow at one side.

When she'd finished pirouetting and heard the adults' lavish praise, she rushed to lean against her father's knee and whisper, "I've new stockings and underthings, too."

Marian was amused to see him flush at her announcement, and glance quickly at herself and Dorothy.

Then it was time for Aurelia to try on her second dress, one selected for Sundays. It was a lovely dress of deep maroon with narrow black velvet ribbon at the neck and cuffs, topped by half-an-inch of stiff ecru lace. The material fell in soft folds from the neck to the hem with no tucks for a waist.

When Aurelia had changed, Marian brushed the girl's hair. The child stood patiently in front of the long mirror in the middle of the dresser and waited for her to complete her task. Marian leaned her head to one side and studied Aurelia's image. "I think I have just the thing in my room to complete your outfit. Wait right here for me. Don't go back to the parlor yet."

She hurried, not certain the girl would listen to her request to wait. When she re-entered the girl's room, puffing slightly from her rush, Aurelia was still there, turning about in front of the mirror, trying to view her new outfit from every angle.

She pinned a large black velvet bow with tiny mauve rosebuds of silk high on one side of Aurelia's fine hair, concentrating hard to pin it securely.

Aurelia gave a small gasp and lifted one hand to touch it lightly. Her small lips open and green eyes wide, she moved closer to the mirror and turned her head to try to better view the bow. Their gazes met in the mirror. "Is this for me?"

Marian smiled at her and nodded. "It's yours for keeps."

Aurelia's gaze slid back to her reflection. "It's pretty." She walked slowly to the door, as though afraid the bow would fall out if she hurried. At the doorway, she turned back. "Aren't you coming?"

Marian nodded again and followed, blinking back sudden tears. The invitation was as close to friendliness as the child had come, and Marian felt a great barrier had tumbled, though she realized actual friendship was still in the future.

When Aurelia showed Everett and Dorothy her new outfit, she made a special effort to point out the bow and explain it was a present from Marian. After she felt sufficient praise had been given the bow and dress, she lifted up one foot and pointed it toward her father, wobbling as she attempted to remain standing on one foot. Her face was screwed up in concentration. "I have new shoes, too. They hurt a little bit, though."

"New shoes are like that. They'll feel better after you've worn them a few times."

Aunt Dorothy stood and offered a thin hand to Aurelia. "You'd best take off your dress before it gets dirty. I'll help you."

The two were still crossing the room when Everett said softly, "Thank you, Miss Ames."

Dorothy stopped at the door and looked back at Everett. Her gaze shifted to Marian. "Since you're living under the same roof, don't you think you might call each other Everett and Marian?"

Marian was grateful her aunt didn't wait for a reply. From the scowl that touched Everett's face, she assumed he wasn't eager to establish a more informal relationship. The thought left her feeling sad, which surprised her. Why should she care what he called her?

"Would it offend you to be called by your Christian name, Miss Ames?"

A smile came instantly to her lips. Even when asking to use her first name, he addressed her formally. "Not at all, Mr. Starr."

His gaze darted to a corner of the room and he bit his lips. She wondered if it was to keep from smiling. He did seem to have an aversion to using the simple, friendly facial expression with her. A moment later he looked at her again, his lips under control. "My name is Everett."

She nodded, trying not to laugh.

He stood and came to stand a foot away from her, plunging his hands into his back pockets. "Thank you for taking Aurelia with you today. I can't recall when I've seen her so happy."

"Every time she's with you," Marian said softly. The words came out before she thought.

A frown dug two creases between his brows. "Excuse me?"

She caught an edge of her bottom lip between her teeth for a moment. "Whenever she's with you, whenever she has all your attention, the child glows with pleasure. She loves you very much."

He grunted and retrieved one hand from his back pocket to rub it along the back of his neck in the manner that was already becoming familiar to her. "Wish I knew how to make her more comfortable with other people."

"Surely that will come with time."

"I don't know. I'd like to think so, but her mother. . ."

He stopped abruptly and Marian frowned. "Losing her mother must have been difficult, but isn't it rather unusual for Aurelia to distrust all young women because of her mother's death?"

"It wasn't her death." Everett's lips thinned. "My wife wasn't a very good mother."

Marian wanted to ask him to expand on his husky admission, to ask whether his wife had truly sent Aurelia away, but she couldn't. They'd known each other such a short time, and not once had he encouraged even the most basic friendly intimacy. When she'd asked Dorothy about Mrs. Starr earlier today, her aunt had pleasantly but firmly changed the subject.

"Well, it's really not your concern, of course."

His brisk admission set embarrassment flaring through her, as though she'd already overstepped the bounds of fledgling acquaintanceship. "No. Forgive me for...intruding. Good night, Everett."

He must have used her own Christian name when he said good night a moment later, but she could have sworn it wasn't Marian he said, but Minnehaha.

five

Everett stood outside the closed door of the kindergarten room, his clenched hands stuffed in the pockets of his short wool overcoat. He shut his eyes and took a deep breath. Sounds of the children joyously singing a nursery rhyme filled the hall.

This is ridiculous. His heart was racing as though he'd just missed being run down by a train, and all because Marian Ames was on the other side of that door. He was reacting to her like a teenage boy, like Jules, who had "encouraged" him to pursue a more personal relationship with Marian.

He had more sense than to do that. No one would know it from the way his heart was acting, though.

He opened his eyes and leaned his shoulder blades against the wall beside the door. He might as well wait for the kids to finish their singing before entering.

Marian had been so sympathetic about Aurelia last night that he'd almost told her about his wife. Good thing he'd stopped after saying his wife hadn't been a good mother.

She hadn't been much of a wife, either. The fact no longer had the power to hurt him. His heart had simply iced over where his wife was concerned. He didn't feel anything anymore; at least not in relation to himself.

The pain his wife had caused their daughter—was *still* causing their daughter—raged inside him. Part of him had wanted to explain to Marian last night, to make her understand everything Aurelia's mother had put her through. And everything *he'd* been put through.

How did a man tell a woman as innocent and pure as Marian that his wife had left him to live with another man without a divorce or benefit of new marriage vows? Or that when the man had been through with her, she went on to be with other men? That she had only returned to her husband and daughter when the illness she'd contracted from one of the men brought her to the brink of death, and there was nowhere else for her to go?

Marian probably didn't know there were women and men in the world who treated each other as shabbily as his wife and those men treated people. He pictured Marian's sweet face, with her sparkling, eager blue eyes and rosy lips that laughed so often and easily, and a physical pain twisted inside of him. He hoped she didn't know anything about such evil.

When his wife returned to their home, sick and broken, there'd never been any question of whether he'd take her back. He was her husband, it was his place to care and provide for her. He knew his neighbors thought him a regular "chump" for not tossing her out on the street, but he believed what he was doing was right.

He'd do the same if given the chance to relive the nightmare, even though his wife never once apologized for leaving or thanked him for taking her back. The fact she'd felt no remorse for the pain she caused him and Aurelia hurt more than her abandonment.

She'd taught him well. Love isn't fair. Life isn't fair. Don't trust people. Don't trust God, either. The lesson left him with a bitter streak. He still believed in God and loving your neighbor. He just didn't believe living by the Golden Rule guaranteed God would reward a person by setting situations right.

The youthful singing stopped, and he straightened. Shifting his shoulders beneath the open coat, he took a deep, steadying breath, and stepped into the room teeming with laughing and squealing four- and five-year-olds.

His gaze swept the room, stopping at Marian. Her back was to him. She was surrounded by a group of children vying with each other for her attention. He could hear her musical laugh above the competing noises.

"Papa!"

Aurelia's happy cry tore his attention from Marian. He knelt and held out open arms to his daughter, catching her in a light hug and apologizing to her silently. He'd never looked for anyone else before looking for her. He'd determined a long time ago he wasn't going to share his heart with anyone but Aurelia. What was he doing seeking Marian?

A soft blue and green plaid flannel skirt suddenly filled the space behind Aurelia. He looked up. Marian smiled down at them. He stood slowly, taking Aurelia's hand in one of his, his gaze glued to Marian's face. He'd just reminded himself he wasn't going to give his heart to a woman and here she was, making his heart race again.

"I thought Aurelia and I would have lunch together." He hadn't meant to sound so abrupt. *Didn't even say hello.*

"What a nice idea! I'm sure she'll be the envy of the other children."

He glanced at her dress. "Is this one of the dresses you bought yesterday?"

Delicate color touched her cheeks. "Yes."

So that was why she had gone shopping yesterday instead of coming to the mission; she'd wanted to purchase a dress that wouldn't set her apart from the other workers or mothers. This wasn't the type of dress she'd normally choose for herself, he was certain. It was too understated, too unfeminine, drew no attention to itself.

It went a long way toward proving he'd been wrong about her, wrong to think she wasn't seriously interested in helping at the mission, wrong to think she was too much of a social butterfly to be involved in something this important and fundamental. Of course, it was only her first day. She might soon tire of it and return to a more frivolous life.

"Would you like to join us for lunch?"

Why had he asked that? He needed to spend more time close to her dizzying influence like he needed another hole in his head!

"Thank you, but I wouldn't think of interfering with Aurelia's special lunch. Besides, all the supervisors are needed to watch the other children."

Disappointment spun through him at her refusal, and he mentally kicked himself. He shouldn't have asked her in the first place, and he had no right being disappointed because she put her duty to the children first.

"We'll see you later then."

Marian nodded a bit distractedly, her attention claimed by a pair of blond-braided girls who looked suspiciously like sisters.

He led Aurelia from the room and toward the cafeteria, only half-hearing her chatter about the morning's activities. He supposed he should be glad about Marian's dress, glad she apparently had more substance than he'd originally guessed. It was stupid to wish she was wearing one of the other garments that seemed such a natural part of her, but he couldn't help remembering the way the blue dress with the lace and flounces which she'd worn yesterday had brought out the blue of her eyes, and made them warmer than the sky in springtime.

≈

Marian was relieved when the blond Johnson sisters broke the emotional rope that tied her to Everett. She'd stared like a schoolgirl at him, not able to think of a thing to say, and wanting to be with them too much to make herself walk away. She was absurdly glad he'd asked her to join them for lunch, although of course she couldn't.

The other kindergarten assistants were back today, over the illnesses that had kept them away the first day Marian had been at the mission. They were all single young women in their late teens or early twenties, and their sincere, eager welcomes made her feel one of them immediately.

Most of the day, Marian assisted Jessie in keeping order among the group of children over which Jessie took charge, following Jessie's lead in the activities. She marveled at the way Jessie and the assistants could take the most ordinary, everyday things and turn them into learning experiences. During the nap time, Jessie explained that every toy and plant and drawing in the room was there for a purpose, that even the different types of balls and blocks were introduced to the children at different stages of learning.

By the end of the day, Marian was sorry it was Friday and the kindergarten wouldn't be operating again until Monday. She definitely found the work with the children stimulating and intriguing. Her heart was filled with thanksgiving to the Lord for the new direction He was giving her life.

❧

Everett stood slowly, lowering the Saturday evening newspaper to his side, and stared in surprise at the tall, lanky young man whom Sonja was showing into the parlor.

"Mr. Paget vill be vaiting for Miss Marian," Sonja informed him briefly before hurrying from the room.

No one had said anything about Marian going out for the evening, Everett thought with a wave of displeasure. He laid the paper on the hassock and stepped forward to offer his hand, sizing the man up quickly and not liking what he saw.

The visitor's hair had a slight reddish tinge that gave just enough color to the underlying white-blond to prevent his egg-shaped head from looking bald. Gold-rimmed round eyeglasses on a straight, thin nose added a touch of color to his otherwise colorless face. Even the mustache was barely noticeable above the small round mouth.

His handshake was firmer than Everett expected. "Philander Paget," he responded to Everett's self-introduction. "I'm escorting Miss Ames to the Charity Ball at the Opera House."

The proprietary tone grated along Everett's nerves. Certainly it must be obvious Paget had no need to assert his position as Marian's escort. Everything about the man's clothes from his gray dress suit with tails to the diamond in his white bowed tie to his crisp linen shirt front fairly shouted money and position.

Everett forced himself to keep from tucking his own shirt more securely into his trousers. As usual, he'd changed immediately upon arriving home from work, exchanging his denim shirt and corduroy trousers for a simple but clean collarless white cotton shirt and brown flannel trousers. He wasn't accustomed to feeling uncomfortable about his dress in what he considered his own home, but he felt so now.

At Everett's reluctant invitation, Philander lowered his long body onto the grandfather's chair with a careful flip of his coat tails. Everett thought irrelevantly that Paget looked perfectly at ease in a chair he himself found too delicate for comfort in spite of its masculine name. He returned to his overstuffed chair and searched for a topic of conversation.

"You're from Minneapolis, I assume?"

The small mouth barely lost its round shape in Paget's smile. "I'm originally from River's Edge. I moved to Minneapolis after receiving my University degree in law."

So he and Marian knew each other from their home town.

Everett leaned an elbow on the wide round chair arm and rested his chin on his fist. "You're a lawyer?"

Paget nodded slightly, a smug look in his pale gray eyes. "I'm with Blatten, Blatten, and Lind."

Everett recognized immediately the name of the most prestigious law firm in the city. Resentment flamed in his chest. It was as though Paget had said, "Beat that, if you can."

"What do you think about the recession?"

One thin shoulder shrugged deliberately. "I believe the economy will soon turn about, if it hasn't already begun to do so. It takes awhile to see verification of financial trends in the market."

"What trends do you think we'll see?"

"Well, as the newspapers said only today, the army of the unemployed is on the decrease."

"Do you believe that?"

"My dear man, of course I believe it. This nation is too strong for an economic depression to keep us in its grip long. You may be sure that nearly all who want work have already secured it."

Chin still on his fist, Everett rubbed his index finger impatiently over his top lip, trying to keep a grip on his temper. He should have known better than to bring up business. He had no patience with uppity wealthy professionals who thought they knew about the world of the normal workingman. Another sign of life's unfair ways.

"If you'll excuse my impertinence, Mr. Paget, I fail to see how anyone can know whether all who wish employment have found work when the city has not endeavored to take a census of the unemployed."

Color flooded the man's normally pale skin until he looked as if he'd been out on one of Minnesota's lakes without a hat on a sunny summer day. "Obviously if there were a great number of men without means of support, people would be begging in the streets for food."

"And you've seen no one doing so?"

"No! Of course not."

Of course not, Everett agreed silently. *Not in the vicinity of the elegant law offices of Blatten, Blatten, and Lind.*

"Mayor Eustis did begin an employment bureau to help the unemployed find positions, you may recall." Paget emphasized his reminder with a nod of his knobby little chin.

"A wise move."

Paget relaxed visibly at Everett's unexpected agreement.

"Do you believe the mayor's bureaus have solved the problem? That there is no shortage of jobs, only difficulty in employer and employee finding each other?"

Paget's thin, white hands spread wide, palms up. "If men are reasonable, yes. They should not expect in these hard times to be employed in the vocation of their preference, or at their usual wages, or perhaps not even a sixty-hour week. If they will accept odd jobs to tide them over, every man who wishes to work may do so."

Everett wondered what Paget would say if someone offered him work on a day-to-day basis doing repairs about their home should he lose his position as an attorney.

His silence must have aggravated Paget, who continued in a ruffled tone. "There is that element of society which is destined to pauperism, that element which chooses not to work, but to subsist on handouts instead."

"So I've been told. Never met one of that element myself."

Paget's tiny mouth opened in protest only to stretch itself slightly into his version of a smile at the sight of Marian entering the room with Dorothy behind her.

Both men shot to their feet.

"Philander!"

Marian's voice was filled with welcome. She moved quickly and gracefully toward her escort, her dainty hands reaching eagerly toward his in greeting. Paget took both hands politely, lifting one to touch the fingers lightly with his lips.

From his attitude one would think it a matter of course with Paget to receive such welcome greetings from lovely young women, Everett thought, jealousy flaming through him.

"You look delightful, Marian. Your gown is exquisite."

He was right about that, Everett thought. He didn't know much about fashion—except that he believed women spent far too much time, worry and money on it—but even he could tell this was an expensive gown.

The dress was of a shiny, rosy-colored material with huge sleeves that emphasized Marian's tiny waist. The lower third of the skirt was embroidered in heavy gold. The neck was high, with a collar that bent out like flower petals just below her chin, framing her perfect, delicate face, and reflecting its color in her cheeks. She wore a sleeveless vest-like garment of dark green velvet trimmed in fur over the gown, which made the color of the dress look all the more feminine.

Paget reached a skinny thumb and forefinger to touch the fur on the side of the vest. "The sable trimming your redingote is the perfect touch."

Sable! Redingote! Imagine a man knowing what to call such things! Everett's arms closed over his chest in disgust. He shifted his feet.

Marian turned at his movement, noticing him for the first time. She smiled her lovely, spontaneous smile, and he felt himself responding to her friendliness as usual.

"Have you and Mr. Paget been introduced, Mr. Starr?"

"We introduced ourselves. Mr. Paget says he's from your home town."

"Yes. I was only a schoolgirl when he went away to University, of course."

Paget touched her elbow. "We should take our leave soon."

"Yes, of course. I believe your hat and cane are in the hall."

Likely he wore one of the popular proper stovepipes, Everett thought bitterly. "Have a pleasant evening, Miss Marian."

Excitement danced in her blue eyes, making her look younger than usual. "Thank you. Good evening."

He didn't follow them to the entryway, but stood where he was, arms still crossed, feeling an unaccustomed restlessness. When he heard the door close behind them, he argued with himself for thirty seconds before stalking to the parlor windows to watch them enter the waiting carriage.

He was right; Paget was wearing the signature stovepipe of

the society gentleman.

What did women see in men like Paget? Stupid question. Money and social position were the obvious answers. Philander Paget was just the type of man his wife had left him for.

He'd hoped Marian was different from most women, that she would not be blinded by a man's money and position. Even though he'd told himself from the beginning that she was born to society and fine living, even though he'd told himself that a woman like Marian could never be for him, he'd hoped she was different.

He snorted, shaking his head at his own foolishness. In spite of all evidence to the contrary, he *still* wanted to believe she was different.

six

The next morning, Aurelia accompanied Marian and Dorothy to church. Marian chided herself for wishing Everett was joining them. He was with the Newsboys' Club Sunday school, however, as Dorothy said he always was on Sunday mornings. Rather than meet in the church, the club met in the basement of the large Syndicate Building downtown.

"Boys being boys, they're more likely to attend if the school isn't located in a church," Aunt Dorothy explained. "So afraid one of the other boys might call them a sissy if they attend a church, you know."

That afternoon Everett's presence seemed to fill the parlor where she and Aunt Dorothy were reading. She put down her book on the history of kindergarten and listened to his answers to Dorothy's questions concerning the Newsboys' Club and the Sunday school. Aurelia leaned against his leg, her gaze glued to his face, listening intently.

Finally Aurelia stretched her little body as far as she could to get closer to his face. "Papa, what shall we do this afternoon?"

He raised his eyebrows and cocked his head. "What would you like to do?"

"I want to go to Minnehaha!"

He laughed and tumbled her hair. "You always want to go there."

She nodded vigorously. "It's my fav'rite place. Can't we go? Ple-e-ease?"

"Well, since you've been such a good girl all week, I guess we can go."

"Oh, thank you, Papa!" Her little arms tried to reach around his waist to give him a squeeze.

"Better change your shoes. Wouldn't want to ruin your new ones."

She started toward the door in a rush, then stopped abruptly. "Are you and Miss Ames coming, Mrs. Dorothy?"

Dorothy looked up from her Bible. "I have some correspondence to complete this afternoon, but I'm sure Marian would enjoy the outing."

Marian met Everett's gaze and wondered what she should reply. She'd always wanted to visit the famous waterfall, but Everett's emotionless face gave no indication whether he would welcome her presence on the outing. "Perhaps Everett and Aurelia would like to spend the afternoon alone together."

Aurelia took a step nearer to Marian and stopped uncertainly. "It's awful pretty there. You can come with us if you want to, Miss Marian."

Aurelia's invitation wasn't accompanied by a smile, and it was given hesitantly, but Marian knew it was sincere. Emotion thickened her throat, and she couldn't reply immediately.

"Please, don't refuse us."

Everett's voice sounded huskier than usual to her, and Marian wondered if he was as surprised as she at Aurelia's invitation.

He always does what's best for his daughter, regardless of his personal distaste in the matter, she thought admiringly.

"I should love to go."

❧

The trolley ride to the falls covered less than five miles. They soon left behind the urban area with its sawmills, flour mills, tall business buildings, and clusters of homes to travel through the sparsely populated countryside. Occasional woods along the way retained their primitive nature, alight with the golden hues of autumn. Everett explained to Marian that the falls they would be visiting were located on Minnehaha Creek, which met the Mississippi River half-a-mile after the creek tumbled over the famous falls.

The grip was crowded with others out to enjoy the sunny, unseasonably warm afternoon, and Marian and Everett were constrained to share a seat, with Aurelia happily taking her place on Everett's lap.

Everett asked whether Marian had enjoyed the charity ball, and she described to him and Aurelia the elaborate decorations, naming many of the social elite who had attended. Aurelia's wide-spaced green eyes were large with wonder when she told of the dancing, the young women's dance cards filled to accommodate the young men who far outnumbered women, the elegant gowns, and the handsome band from nearby Fort Snelling.

Certain her chattering wasn't the least interesting to Everett, she changed the topic. "Philander introduced me to Mayor Eustis and County Commissioner Dyer last evening. Mr. Dyer said the employment outlook for the nation is bright, and within two months, the country will be in a position to employ every man who is seeking work."

It looked to her as though he was trying hard not to sneer and failing miserably. "I'm sure Paget agreed with that wholeheartedly. What did the mayor say to it?"

She grinned. "Like a true politician, he neither agreed or disagreed. He certainly did not commit himself to a time period. He said when the money scare is over and the currency back into circulation, commerce would move again. Also, that neither hunger or cold will come to any unemployed man of the city."

His firm lips compressed and his rich brown eyes darkened. "Fool politicians." Then his lips relaxed somewhat. "For a woman, you remember a great deal of a business conversation."

Anger flared bright and spontaneous. She tilted her head

slightly to one side and opened her eyes wide. "Was that intended as a compliment, Mr. Starr?"

The grin she so liked and saw all too seldom split his face. "Yes, it was, actually. Was it difficult to spot?"

"It was rather qualified, don't you think? Though not so decidedly rude as Philander's statement to Mayor Eustis last evening." She lifted her chin and gave an imitation of Philander looking down his skinny nose. "'Women's little attempts at understanding business are quite amusing, are they not?'"

She hoped the laughter in Everett's eyes was at her imitation of Philander's voice and manner, and not in sympathy with Philander's statement.

"I assume you responded to his. . .attack?"

She fidgeted in the seat. "I ignored the next dance for which he'd signed my card."

He grinned broadly. "What did you do to bring about his unflattering comment?"

She pretended indignation. "Well, I like that! What makes you assume it was me and not some other lady making the terrible breach of speaking business with men at a social engagement?"

"Just a hunch."

"I mentioned the mission, the work being accomplished there, and the financial problems of some of the families using the mission's services."

She kept to herself Philander's later comments when they had been alone, to the effect that when a young man's lady friend or wife was involved in charity work it reflected well on her escort or husband. He'd expressed a hope she'd continue her work at the mission. She'd told him hotly that whether she continued would not be determined by her concern for his career aspirations.

The trolley rolled to a stop at Minnehaha Park, and people impatiently filed from the grip into the glorious, mild autumn day.

They could hear the falls before they saw them, though the sound wasn't unduly loud. It was necessary to descend the bluff by a flight of wide stone steps in order to view the famous sight. Though she kept one gloved hand on the thin railing while descending and lifted her skirt with the other to keep from tripping on the rough-hewn steps, Everett kept his fingers at her elbow for her safety. His touch was far more unsettling than the steep steps!

At the bottom, a wooden walking bridge spanned the creek, a rough log railing on each side. There were a number of other viewers on the steps, bridge, and surrounding area, but at her first sight of the falls, Marian forgot them all. In the midst of the bridge, she clutched the wooden rail and stared in wonder at the sixty-foot fall of water dancing in the sunlight that filtered through the baring autumn branches. It fell as straight as a bride's veil.

"'Where the Falls of Minnehaha flash and gleam among the oak trees, laugh and leap into the valley,'" she whispered, her gaze drinking in the beauty before her.

"Did you memorize the poem in school?"

Everett's amused question drew her gaze to his. He stood beside her, leaning against the rail.

"Yes. You, too?"

He nodded. "Minnehaha, Laughing Water."

He wasn't looking at the waterfall as he repeated its name. He was looking into her eyes, with a dreamy look she'd never seen in his strong, usually sober face.

Aurelia slipped between them, gripping one of the lower logs that crisscrossed between the railing and the bridge forming a picturesque barrier between the visitors and the water. Marian breathed a soft sigh of relief as Aurelia's presence broke the power that had bound her gaze to Everett's.

Aurelia leaned forward, intent on the waterfall, and her

broad-brimmed hat was knocked back by the log railing. Everett caught it as it fell, but Aurelia didn't notice it was missing. He smiled broadly at her absorption, and shared a look of laughter with Marian. The look was so unconsciously friendly that it warmed her with its intimacy.

She reached to smooth a lock of Aurelia's hair. "No wonder this is your favorite spot. It's beautiful."

Aurelia graced her with a timid smile, but sidled closer to her father as she did so. Marian wondered whether she would ever gain the child's trust.

They stood together in mutual admiration for the exquisite beauty of God's creation, enjoying the relaxing sound of the water.

Eventually Aurelia said reflectively, without taking her gaze from the mesmerizing falls, "Why doesn't Minnehaha Falls run out of water?"

Everett and Marian exchanged amused glances over her head.

"Because a river keeps bringing water to it," Everett explained.

Aurelia pushed her chin against the railing and scowled in concentration, studying the falls harder than ever. "But what if the river stops?"

Her father rubbed one large hand comfortingly over her shoulder blades. "It won't stop unless men build a dam, and that won't happen, because people like the falls too much."

"Oh."

Aurelia darted off to climb down the bank and sit on a protruding rock, watching the creek flow by. Without her presence, Marian grew uncomfortable beside Everett. More to dispel her uneasiness than for any other reason she said, "It's not a very loud waterfall."

"No," he agreed. "Not like the Falls of St. Anthony near the mission. In 1766, the Englishman, Jonathan Carver, claimed those falls could be heard fifteen miles through the wilderness.

Of course, they are significantly tamed now that Minneapolis' industrial interests have converted the falls into a staid power source."

She didn't reply. His dislike for those industrial powers was clearly revealed in his strained voice. Her uncle, Aunt Dorothy's husband, had owned one of the sawmills that used that power. She'd argued with him once before over the benefits of industry. She had no intention of destroying the beauty of this day with another useless disagreement.

He leaned his elbows on the railing, the brown of his jacket dark against the bleached, peeled wood, his tall frame bent almost in half. "The Indians called the Falls of St. Anthony *Minnerara*."

She smirked and gave him a derisive glance. "I am not so gullible as to believe that."

"It's true. The word means 'curling water' in the Sioux language. The land around the falls was holy ground to many Indian nations. To fish, hunt, or camp there was to commit sacrilege. Then Fort Snelling was built downriver, and, soon after, people began using the falls for power. Today the curling water is a smooth cascade running industries."

He was back to the same topic.

"Perhaps we're like the river," she ventured more cautiously than was her custom. "Minnehaha Falls is lovely in its wild state. The Falls of St. Anthony have lost their pristine beauty, but tamed for man's use, they are the financial foundation of the city. If we let Him, God can tame our selfish natures for His use, also."

He cast her a sideways glance, but didn't respond as a young, starry-eyed couple stopped beside them, exclaiming over the falls. Marian and Everett remained silent until they walked on.

"Strange," Everett said, avoiding reference to her theory, "that Minnehaha Falls should be revered for an Indian tale created by a white man, and the Indian stories surrounding the Falls of St. Anthony are all but unknown."

"What stories?"

"The Spirit Island story for one. There are many versions of it, but basically it tells of the Indian woman, *Ampato Sapa,* Dark Day. She was crushed when her brave took a second wife. In her despair, she placed their infant child in her canoe, and paddled over the falls, killing them both. The Indians believed her spirit rose in the spray at the small island at the foot of the falls."

"How awful!"

One corner of his mouth lifted in the beginning of a smile. "Most people consider the story romantic."

"What is romantic about such timidity?"

He turned to fully face her, astonishment in every line of his face. "Timidity?"

"Of course! You are far more courageous than Dark Day."

He appeared to grapple for her meaning. "Excuse me?"

Embarrassment flooded her. "I'm afraid I spoke before I thought. It's one of my many faults, as you might have noticed."

"What did you mean?"

"Only that upon the loss of your wife, you didn't kill yourself and Aurelia. You chose the more difficult but far more courageous path of life."

Now what had she said to cause him to look like a thunderstorm planning to crash about her? "Of course, Dark Day's brave was only disloyal, and your wife. . .is. . .gone." Her voice trailed off. "I'm making a dreadful mess of this. Please forgive me."

His eyes raked hers.

Then suddenly, Aurelia was there, snapping the tension between them.

Marian watched Everett struggle to shove away the anger

that was so inexplicable to her.

The child looked up at her father. "Papa, can we show Miss Ames our other waterfall?"

Marian wondered at the surprise that passed over his face before his brows drew together slightly. "Are you sure you want to?"

Aurelia nodded vigorously.

He settled her hat on her head. "Then lead the way."

She darted across the bridge and into the foliage along the creek leading away from the falls. Everett offered his hand stiffly to Marian as they followed her, Marian lifting her skirt carefully to protect it from the innocent looking branches of the small bushes and plants. It was only a few feet before they came to a faded, narrow path.

Everett released her hand once they were upon the path. Disappointment surged through Marian, but he leaned close to say, "You must have won her trust. She's always considered these our secret falls, though we share the knowledge of them with many nearby residents."

She must be making more progress with the child's affections than she'd thought. It left a pleasant glow within her as she followed Aurelia through the wild glen.

Suddenly Aurelia stopped, looking behind her to assure herself Marian and Everett had arrived also. She dropped to her knees, heedless of her new gown and stockings, and pointed to a low, tiny tumble of water. "Look!"

"Why, it's lovely!" Marian settled carefully beside the girl.

"Tell her what the fall is called, Aurelia."

She looked at Marian, and for the first time since they'd met, the girl's face was alight with genuine joy that caught at Marian's heart. "Minnegiggle!"

Marian laughed aloud. "What an appropriate name."

"Yes." Aurelia giggled. Her tiny teeth flashed before she covered her mouth with her chubby fingers, her green eyes continuing to dance. Marian wanted to hug Aurelia to her, but knew better than to press her advantage at this first tenuous branch of friendship.

When they finally started back, Aurelia again took the lead, heading into the thick foliage as though it were her natural element. *Indeed,* Marian thought, *the girl was more at ease here than among the children at the kindergarten, and definitely more so than among any adults—other than her father, of course.*

At the bridge, Marian stopped to admire the falls once more, loath to leave their sparkling, tranquil beauty. Aurelia stood at one side of her, Everett at the other.

What a different world from the mission, Washington Avenue and the built-up Mississippi riverside!

Impulsively, she turned to Everett. "Thank you for allowing me to share your day. I know Sunday afternoons are your special times with Aurelia, and I have intruded upon that. The falls are so lovely. I shall always treasure this day."

Something stirred deep in the eyes meeting her gaze. His voice was low when he replied, and the timbre in it set her pulse dancing. "It's I who should thank you. Aurelia hasn't been like this with a young woman since her mother—well, not for a long time."

His love and concern for his daughter caught at her heart. She wanted to put her arms around him and comfort him for all the pain he'd been through with his wife and daughter, and the desire shook her intensely. Why did this man reach emotions deep within her which no other man had touched?

"I think she is only beginning to heal." Her answer was low also, in hopes of keeping her words from Aurelia's hearing, and her voice shook with the knowledge of her feelings for this man.

"At least the healing finally *has* started."

Swallowing her fears, she lightly touched the arm of his

jacket. "I'm sure your love will complete the healing. It takes time."

She dropped her hand, turning from him toward the falls once more, hoping he hadn't seen the intensity of her feelings reflected in her face.

"I would have thought you too young to know how long it takes a heart to heal."

Was there a touch of sarcasm in his statement? A smile pulled at her lips. If she told him that within the last two months she'd been engaged to two men, one of them an outlaw, and been kidnapped, then caught in a shoot-out between outlaws and Pinkerton detectives, would he still think her so young? She knew the thought added a saucy sparkle to her eyes when she looked back at him.

"You think me a child, Mr. Starr?"

"Hardly!" The look that accompanied his husky exclamation sent shivers through her. "But you are quite young, and inexperienced with life's troubles."

For a moment she was tempted to tell him of her recent past, just to show how wrong he was about her, but she found suddenly that she didn't want him to know the truth. She didn't want to see the disillusionment in his eyes upon hearing she'd been engaged to an outlaw, no matter what the justification. Besides, until Justin had broken their engagement two months earlier, she *had* been inexperienced with life's troubles.

"Appearances can be deceiving," she said quietly.

Without waiting for the others, she started toward the stairs. She was suddenly eager to get back to her aunt's home, eager to be alone with her thoughts so she could examine this strange attraction that was growing for Everett.

seven

Marian said good-bye to the last child to leave the mission for the day, and began clearing small piles of clay from one of the tables. Glancing at the children's primitive modeling efforts proudly displayed upon a wall shelf, she smiled. It was Friday, and the end of her first entire week at the Kindergarten and Industrial Association. It had been the most satisfying, exciting, and contented week of her life, regardless that most people would think such emotions could not be concurrent.

She formed the remainder of the pliable gray material into a lumpy ball and placed it in a tin. Wiping her hands on a small towel, she crossed to where Miss Watkins was neatly piling cardboard sewing cards. "After watching me this week, are you still willing to accept me into the kindergarten teacher training?"

A grin spread across Jessie's wide, plain face. "I was hoping you would wish to join. I've never seen a woman who has a greater heart for the children."

Marian released a shaky breath. "I never realized that kindergarten was more than a supervised playroom. You've taught me so much already about the way children learn, and how important the right toys—I mean, gifts—are to a child's development. It's so exciting."

"It's only the beginning. You'll soon see how much we can do for the children to ready them for the primary grades and to face life's sometimes difficult experiences. That's what is truly exciting about this work."

Marian took a cloth from the pail of water kept in the room for cleaning purposes, and began wiping the table where the children had created their clay figures. "Aunt Dorothy told me you live upstairs here."

"Yes," Jessie replied cheerfully, lifting a chair to a table top to begin readying the room for the daily sweeping.

"Do you find it frightening, staying here alone?"

"I'm not alone. One of my assistants, lives here, too."

"I mean, alone without a man in the house. I've never lived in a house where there wasn't a man."

Jessie's low laugh rippled out. "I'm afraid it would cast an unsightly shadow upon the mission's reputation should a man live here with two single women."

A smile tugged at Marian's lips. "It might at that."

"Besides, no one would hurt us. We're part of the community, working *with* them, not *for* them. I hope we always shall be. Working here or at some similar house is all I wish to do in life."

Marian straightened, the damp cloth still in her hand. "You mean that you wish to dedicate your life to your work?"

"Yes."

"Don't you wish to marry?"

Jessie's hands rested on the bowed back of the little chair she'd just placed on the table, and a small smile formed on her wide lips for a moment. "I believe both a vocation and a family require all of a woman's efforts, and therefore don't believe them compatible. I'm sure a marriage and family would be wonderful, but I wouldn't want to give up teaching or being part of this or a similar community for them."

Marian finished her work in silence. She'd heard there were many college-educated women who felt that way today, but she'd never met any. As much as she enjoyed working with the children in the kindergarten, she couldn't imagine her life without a husband and children of her own.

It was only a few short weeks ago she'd recommitted her life to God, after Justin had broken their engagement and she'd made such a mess of everything. Already she'd seen signs of His work in her life, trying to peel the layers of self-absorption from her heart.

She'd never bothered much in the past for anything beyond her own pleasure. Her experience with Justin had shown her that unflattering fact about herself. Now she'd been introduced to the mission and the kindergarten work, and she believed it was God Who had placed in her heart the longing to become more fully involved in the work.

Was Jessie correct in her belief that a woman could not devote herself to both teaching and a family? Her stomach tightened painfully. Would God require her to give up the dream of a husband and children? Was that another change He would make in her life?

When she'd decided to put God first in her life, it had never occurred to her that He might ask anything so difficult, anything that might actually be painful for her to endure. For the first time, she dreaded discovering what He might ask of her, for whatever it might be, she had no intention of saying *no* to Him.

⁂

Everett shoved his shoulders deeper into the back of the overstuffed chair in the corner of the parlor and glared over the top of the Sunday *Minneapolis Tribune* at Philander Paget, seated across the room giving his whole-hearted attention to Marian.

Paget had spent every Sunday afternoon in this parlor since their Minnehaha outing almost two months earlier, and Everett was getting downright tired of seeing his smug, privileged face. Not that he had anything in particular against the man, except his interest in Marian.

Or more to the point, Marian's interest in him.

Of course, he didn't care for the man's politics, either.

His gaze slid to Marian, and the now familiar ache began in

his chest. The gentle curve of the divan's carved rosewood border made a perfect backdrop for her. The sapphire-blue gown she wore deepened the blue of her eyes, and elaborate trimmings complimented her in a way the simple frocks she wore at the mission never did.

Mrs. Dorothy sat beside her reading, occasionally joining in the couple's conversation. He'd be eternally grateful for the simple, gracious manner in which she'd invited him and Aurelia into her home.

If it weren't for Aurelia, he'd leave here in spite of Mrs. Dorothy's kindnesses. Even if he thought for a moment that a young woman with Marian's upbringing would be interested in him, he wouldn't consider trying to court her. That being the case, living under the same roof with her was growing more painful each day.

Yet he couldn't help himself from seeking her presence. Right now, for instance, he didn't have to read the paper here, with the sight of Paget giving Marian his attentions grating on his nerves. He could read the paper in the kitchen or his bedchamber instead.

It was so good to be around Marian, though, just to be able to look on her sweet beauty and hear her lovely voice and laugh. So good, and so painful.

His initial attraction to Marian had deepened into admiration. She hadn't grown tired of the mission, but devoted herself to the free kindergarten and Mothers' Meetings. She shared with him and Dorothy the knowledge gained in the Kindergarten teacher training. It both amused and touched him when she spoke of the importance of a parent's habits on a child, and what elements a child needed for a happy home life. With sweet tact, she avoided mentioning the need for a loving mother.

Paget's high-pitched voice brought Everett out of his reflections.

Paget sat in the fancy grandfather chair, his usual place, in his gray cashmere suit, his knees crossed casually, looking all too much at home for Everett's pleasure. Marian responded with a laugh to something Paget said, and he looked smugly pleased with himself.

Everett dug his nose into the newspaper, trying to force an interest in the world outside the parlor. However, he was open to the society page, and the first thing his glance fell upon was a description of the Christmas party Paget and Marian had attended the night before.

Biting back a mutter of disgust, he noisily and hastily turned the offending page. He'd never bothered to pause over the society pages until Paget had begun escorting Marian. Now every Sunday he sought out descriptions of the entertainments they attended together, along with the listing of the social elite with whom they hobnobbed. Stupid thing to do. It only depressed or angered him.

"Heard there was another fire set at the World's Fair exhibition buildings in Chicago." Paget's voice invaded Everett's self-imposed barrier. "Fortunately there was little damage. Not the first incendiary attempt there, and probably won't be the last. The Exhibition was extraordinary. Did you visit it, Marian?"

Everett strained to hear her reply. It was a moment before she answered.

"No. Justin and I planned to attend on our honeymoon, but then he married Constance, of course."

Shock whipped through Everett like a sudden winter blizzard across the prairie. She'd been engaged! Some incredibly fortunate man had had Marian's promise to be his wife, and chose to marry another!

The news filled his thoughts, and he didn't notice Paget's colorful description of the Columbian Exhibition held that year in Chicago.

The thought of anyone hurting Marian constricted his chest like a band of iron and brought out the protective male in him.

He recalled Mrs. Dorothy had planned a trip early this fall to attend a wedding, then had cancelled her plans at the last minute. The bridegroom had married someone else two days before the wedding. Could that have been Marian's wedding? He'd never considered the possibility. Marian was too lovely for any man to leave at the altar.

Had she loved the man madly? Foolish question! Why else agree to marry him?

What had this Justin been like? What kind of man would she love?

He'd accused her more than once of not knowing anything of life's uglier side, yet she'd evidently been betrayed by love as he had. Why hadn't it turned her bitter, resentful, distrustful as it had made him?

"Read about the mayor's soup kitchen, Starr?"

Paget's comment dragged Everett back from his thoughts. He grimaced, reluctantly lowering the newspaper until he could see Paget. The man was leaning slightly forward in his chair, one arm akimbo with his hand on his knee, a saucy grin on his skinny face.

"Yes, I read it."

The almost colorless eyebrows rose above the round gold eyeglasses. "Well? What do you think of it?"

"It's a commendable action, but not enough."

Paget reared back. "What do you mean, not enough? A free bowl of soup to every unfortunate homeless man staying at the police station nights, and it's not enough?"

"Think you'd like to live on one bowl of soup a day?"

"It's not just broth, there's vegetables and breads in it."

"Not much to keep a man alive."

"'Beggars can't be choosers,' as they say."

"No, apparently not." Everett shifted his attention to Sonja, who was replacing an almost empty crystal plate on the small marble-topped table beside Paget with a plate filled with delicate, fancy cookies. The corners of her mouth were pulled back so tightly they dented her thick cheeks. "What do you think of the soup kitchen, Sonja?"

Her eyes widened in surprise. "It is not for me to say, sir."

"I don't know why not. I'm sure you, like the rest of us, know people out of work because of the recession."

She still hesitated.

Marian leaned forward slightly. "Tell us what you think."

Sonja's back straightened and her elbows rested on her wide hips. "*Mormor* alvays said, 'Ven gruel comes raining down, the poor vun has no spoon.'"

Paget barked a short laugh. "And what is that piece of drivel supposed to mean?"

Sonja lifted her double chin and gave him a scathing look. "The vise don't need proverbs explained to them."

It was all Everett could do to keep back a cheer. He glanced back at Marian. She was diligently fingering a piece of lace running down one side of her gown, as though studying a possible tear, and he knew she was holding back a laugh, too. Truth told, he wasn't certain himself how Sonja's grandmother's proverb applied to the present situation, but he wouldn't admit it to Paget for all the money in the world. He forced his attention back to Sonja.

"Many of the Svedish people here are out of vork. Ve started a Svedish-American Union last year to help our people in hard times. Vun of my family's neighbors is in the Union, und he says the Union is starting its own labor and assistance bureau to help Svedes. It is needed, too." She nodded her head so emphatically that her cheeks bounced. "The Stockholm newspaper says those in Sveden who receif money from husbands und sons in America are receifing no money now, because our people can't find vork."

Paget linked his skinny fingers about one knee and tried unsuccessfully to look down his nose at the broad-shouldered woman towering above him. "The aldermen have proposed a plan to hire the unemployed to clean streets and remove snow from sidewalks."

Sonja relented somewhat. "*Ja. That is so. The city has done* a little. My brother-in-law is one of de fifty men hired to macadamize University Boulevard."

Marian's mouth opened in surprise. "I didn't know you had relatives out of work because of the hard times."

"*Ja.*" The large shoulders shrugged beneath her black dress. "Doesn't everyone?"

Obviously Marian still isn't aware of the extent of the problem, Everett thought.

"A number of the children in the mission kindergarten have unemployed fathers," he said quietly.

Her troubled gaze met his. "I'm glad we can help them by caring for and training their children."

Paget's small mouth pursed in derision. "I hardly think watching their children a few hours each day is a great help to unemployed men."

Her eyes sparked blue fire, and Everett was glad to see her angry with the pompous man.

"Some of the mothers work, if the fathers can't. Jessie Watkins says it helps the parents to know their children are safely cared for and have at least one warm meal each day. I: helps the children, too. Froebel believes even play can help the child prepare for difficulties later in life."

Everett smiled. She'd been quoting Froebel, the "Father of Kindergarten," incessantly since beginning the training course for kindergarten teachers. "What does the brilliant man say this time?"

"He believes children should be trained to meet difficulties, and not be sheltered from them. Even in play, he says—" she paused and reached for the book she'd been reading when Paget had arrived, turned the pages until she came to the place she sought. "He says, 'Through play, in which he is watched over by your love, and protected by your care, your baby increases both his strength and his consciousness of strength. The consciousness of strength can come only by being helped over and over again to meet difficulties, both physical and spiritual.'"

"Nonsense."

Marian half rose in protest at Paget's dismissal, but Everett interrupted. "So when a child learns to finally master an area of play, the accomplishment strengthens him and makes him less afraid to face difficulties later in life?"

"Yes, exactly!"

Excitement flashed in Marian's eyes. Everett loved to watch that excitement, which was common when she read Froebel or one of the other experts on teaching children. Her eagerness for children's possibilities was a thing of beauty in his eyes, and love for children lit her from within.

She leaned forward eagerly, the book still open in her hand. "Froebel calls the toys children use in kindergarten 'gifts.' I didn't understand his reasoning at first, but I think I do now. They are gifts because through them a child learns how to deal with the challenges life offers. By discovering the best use for a toy, or gift, they learn the freedom of success and enjoyment in spite of limitation. He believes one's life is enriched by making the most of things within their limitations. That is, by discovering that it's not what we have that makes life rich, but how we use what we have."

It was something his wife had never learned, Everett thought. She'd chafed under limitations, struggled against them all her short life, believing freedom lay in lack of constraints, either moral or financial. Sadness flooded his chest. In the end, her denial of the constraints had killed her.

His gaze rested on Marian's face, so full of life and innocent-appearing beauty, and compared it in his mind to his wife's in the last years of her too-short life. His wife had looked worn and old toward the end, the ravages of the life she'd chosen all too clear in the texture and wrinkles of her once pretty face. Her eyes weren't full of the exciting possibilities life offered, but were dull or flashing in turn with bitterness, anger, and disillusionment.

"I dare say Minneapolis' unemployed men would find difficulty looking upon the Economic Depression of 1893 as a gift." Philander's voice dripped disdain.

"You miss the point, Philander. The children's kindergarten experiences may benefit them when they face their own problems as adults."

From the smirk on the man's face, Everett didn't think Paget was convinced.

Marian sighed, and rubbed a palm fondly over the book's brown leather cover. "I do wish Minneapolis would add kindergarten to the public school system, like St. Paul has done. The free kindergartens in the city reach so few children. All children should have its benefits."

"Not much chance of that happening soon," commented Everett. "The city is having difficulty enough funding the school programs already established. The recession is making everything in the city budget difficult to pay for."

"We finally agree on something, Starr." Paget gave him a conspiratorial wink. "We might not agree on how the city should spend its funds, but we agree they shouldn't be spent on nurseries."

Marian fairly shot to her feet. The knuckles of her delicate hand clutching the book were white against the brown binding.

Everett rose also. He wasn't about to be included in her anger. "Wrong again, Paget. I never think it's foolish to spend money on our city's children. That said, I'm off to locate my own child."

Marian flashed him a look of gratitude that sent a twist of

delight through him.

He'd barely reached the hall when he heard Marian say to Paget, "The kindergarten movement is important to me, and I'll not listen to you belittle it. I am sorely tempted to tell you exactly what I think of your attitude. Therefore, I request that you permit me to remain a lady by drawing this visit to a close."

Everett continued down the hall and out of reach of their voices.

Strange, at first he'd told himself she was too innocent for a man like himself to love. Now that he knew of her broken engagement, he was wishing she had never had to experience pain.

Only love could make a man so wishy-washy.

He stopped cold. *He was falling in love with Marian.* He clenched his teeth to keep back a groan and felt sweat break out on his brow.

He was really in trouble now.

eight

With difficulty, Marian slipped one more basket handle over Jules' arm. He grinned merrily and sidled through the mission's front door Everett held for him. A bracing winter's chill followed Everett from the door to the pile of baskets and clothing in the hall.

Marian continued piling large baskets together as much as possible. "Didn't Jessie have a wonderful idea, using the mission for a collection point? I wonder whether all of these baskets, clothes, and money would have been donated for the mayor's relief effort if the neighbors had had to take them to City Hall or a patrol station."

Everett pushed a pile of worn flannel trousers into one of the larger baskets. "Too much of this was donated by people who need it themselves."

"Doubtless it pleases them to give to others as much as it pleases you." She allowed him no chance to respond. "Personally, I find it thrilling to think the people of the city are responding so eagerly to Mayor Eustis' request for donations. A basket of food for each unemployed family on Christmas." She sent him a teasing glance from beneath her lashes. "Surely even you must agree that's a fine thing."

Jules and a fellow Newsboys' Club member entered while he answered, "Too bad it took the Christmas season to bring out the 'good will to men.' Likely as soon as Christmas Day is past, the city's concern for the unemployed will pass with it."

Aware of the boys' presence, Marian held her temper. When the door swung shut beyond them once more, she turned on Everett, letting her impatience flash. "You make me tired!

You've been complaining for months over the state of the unemployed, and now that something is being done for them, you continue to complain!"

Everett grasped one of the handles and swung a basket toward her. His brown eyes spit fire. "One basket of food for an entire family. Some flour, rice, butter, a couple pounds of beef, a can of oysters, and some Christmas candy for the youngsters. How long do you think that will feed a family?"

Her nails bit into the palms of her hands. "A good deal longer than nothing."

"The city's been searching out the unemployed for less than two weeks, and already they have eight hundred families on their Christmas basket list. They estimate those families include about six thousand people. More *must* be done."

"At least the city has finally begun a census of the unemployed, and the citizens are becoming aware of the great need. It's a beginning."

"It should have been done months ago. You think I complain too much. I don't understand how you can be satisfied with the little being done."

Jules' laugh came through the door, and Marian dropped her voice to a loud, angry whisper. "The Newsboys' Club members look up to you. The least you can do is give the impression you approve of the Mayor's Christmas basket program."

His square jaw set stubbornly, but when Jules and his friend came inside a moment later, he managed a smile and slapped Jules on the back. "Good job you two are doing. Appreciate your coming out in the cold to deliver these to City Hall."

Jules shrugged his shoulders uneasily beneath his worn wool coat, and his friend ducked his head with an embarrassed grin.

"Aw, it's not so much," Jules mumbled. He dragged a handful of coins from his pocket and held it out to Marian. "The Newsboys wanted ta donate some money for the Christmas baskets."

"How kind of you!" She accepted graciously, though she

suspected some of the Newsboys' families would be among those receiving baskets. Opening the large red coffee tin on the hall desk, she dropped the coins inside. It was already heavy with other donations.

She held it out to Jules. "Would you deliver this to City Hall along with the baskets and clothes?"

He accepted it, flushing with pride at her trust.

Minutes later the boys' arms were piled with the last of the donations. "Comin' with us?" Jules asked Everett.

Everett shook his head. "It's dark out. I'll be seeing Miss Ames home."

Jules grinned. "Tough job."

Everett yanked Jules' hat over his eyes and pushed him through the door.

"I can see myself home if you'd like to go with them," Marian offered.

"They aren't alone. It's Sonja's brother's wagon, you might recall, and he's driving the team. Besides, it isn't wise for women to walk the city alone after dark," Everett insisted.

Five minutes later their shoulders were bent against the raw December wind. It cut through Marian's thick cape, tugged at the ends of her soft muffler, and set her teeth chattering. Her eyes and nose stung from the sharp chill.

Everett moved from her left to her right side and he became an intentional buffer for her from the wind, his shoulder almost touching hers.

"Thank you."

He didn't answer. In spite of an occasional street lamp, it was too dark to distinguish his features beneath his soft slouch hat. It was too early for the stars and moon to add their light, though it was a clear night.

Perhaps it was the cover of darkness that gave Everett the courage to broach such a personal topic, she reflected later.

"Marian, I owe you an apology."

She gave him a quick sideways smile, knowing he couldn't

see it in the dark. "More than one, most likely."

"Yes, well, one in particular."

They walked another ten steps in silence.

"You're forgiven."

"But I haven't said anything!"

"At this rate, you never shall. Besides, I can't think of anything you've done which I find unforgivable."

"This was only in my mind. When we met, I thought you were unfamiliar with the hard things of life, and it was for that reason you were always so happy."

"You've mentioned my inexperience before."

She slipped on an unexpected spot of ice, and his arm caught her about her waist. He drew her close, supporting her over the treacherous stretch of lumpy frozen snow and ice.

When they'd traversed the difficult area, his arm remained. Its presence set her pulse quick-stepping, though she suspected it remained because they were both warmer this way.

"When Paget was visiting Sunday," he continued in a strained voice most unlike his usual deep rumble, "you mentioned your engagement."

Her breath almost stopped. She hadn't realized until that moment how comfortable it was to be around people who didn't know of her past. "Yes?"

"From what you said, I gather your fiancé married another woman."

"Yes, two days before we were to be married."

His steps faltered. His arm drew her closer. "I'm sorry," he whispered just above her ear.

She bent her head until the small brim of her hat slipped between them. She didn't want pity.

"You know what it's like to lose someone you love. That's the injustice I did you, Marian, believing your life had always been easy."

"I expect you felt your loss deeper than I felt the loss of Justin. You shared many years and a child with your wife."

Half a block passed before he spoke again. "Why aren't you bitter? Most women in your situation would be filled with resentment."

"For the first few weeks, anger consumed my life."

"What happened to change you?"

"I acted very foolishly, and had my revenge."

"Did the act of revenge leave you with a sense of justice that you're no longer angry?"

"No. In exacting my childish revenge, I hurt many people, myself included. I realized then what a selfish person I'd become. I asked the Lord to forgive me, and recommitted my life to Him."

"Didn't the unfairness of it all make you angry with God?"

"Perhaps at first. Being angry didn't change the fact that Justin was out of my life forever. I needed to put my energies into living life as it is, not as I'd thought it would be. Besides, I expect I was too selfish to make Justin a good wife. I had much to learn about loving."

They walked up the steps to her aunt's porch, his arm slipping from her back when she turned to face him. Light from the hall shone through the etched glass of the door, making planes of light and shadow of his face. "You lost a wife, and Aurelia lost a mother. I wish neither of you had had to experience that. I'm so very sorry she's no longer with you."

She couldn't read the expression in his eyes, but she sensed the tenseness in his jaw.

He turned to open the door. "As you said, one has to live life as it is."

❧

The next morning Marian packed for her trip to Rivers' Edge and her parents' home for Christmas. *Two weeks away from the kindergarten, Jessie Watkins, Aunt Dorothy, and Aurelia,* she thought in despair.

And Everett. She lowered the top of her trunk with a soft "thunk." The thought of not seeing him every day made her chest feel it was being slowly crushed. What was it going to be like in actuality?

When she'd told the Lord a few months ago she wanted to live for Him instead of herself, she hadn't known He would make such sweeping changes in her life! She used to live only for her own pleasure. Now her life was wrapped up with fifty kindergarten children and their families, Aunt Dorothy, Aurelia, and Everett.

She dabbed scent on her wrists with the stopper of the crystal perfume bottle. The fragrance of lilacs filled the room with springtime.

"Ready for me to take that trunk down?"

Marian started at Everett's voice. She swung around, warmth surging up her neck and over her face. He'd never been in her bedchamber before, and his presence there made her feel especially vulnerable. To avoid looking at him she reached for the small, silver-handled alligator satchel she'd be carrying on the railroad car. "Yes, I've completed my packing."

"Marian—"

He hesitated, and she opened the satchel, muddling about in it unnecessarily. He'd hardly spoken two words to her today. He was probably embarrassed over the personal discussion they'd had last evening.

"I'd like to ask you a favor."

He stated the fact so quickly the words almost ran together. *He must be as uncomfortable as I am.* The thought slightly elevated her courage, but she refused to face him yet.

"It's Aurelia. She's upset over your leaving. I wonder if you'd speak with her?"

She snapped the bag shut and finally faced him. "Of course. I couldn't leave without saying goodbye to her."

The lines about his mouth relaxed, and his shoulders lowered slightly, as though they'd been tensed against her possible refusal. "Thank you. She's. . .she's afraid you won't return."

Not return! Never see Everett again! The possibility shot terror through her.

She removed an album covered with emerald green plush from her ladies' desk, and proceeded him through the door, trying to ignore the tingles that danced along her nerves at passing so close that her navy traveling outfit's wide sleeves brushed his jacket.

Aurelia was in the parlor, curled into a corner of the rose brocade divan, her green eyes sparkling with unshed tears. Marian thought her heart would break open at the child's obvious care for her. To think she'd believed Aurelia still indifferent to her after two months of trying to win her love and confidence.

She knelt before the divan and blinked tears from her own eyes. "I'm leaving in a few minutes to spend Christmas with my mother and father." She smiled tremulously. "You'll be spending Christmas with your father, too, won't you?"

Aurelia nodded slowly. "Why don't your mother and father come here for Christmas?"

Marian wished they would! "They've spent all their Christmases at their house in River's Edge. I think they'd be lonely for it if they spent this Christmas elsewhere." She held the thick album out to the little girl. "Would you do me a favor while I'm gone? Would you take care of my album? I wouldn't want anything to happen to it while I'm away, you see."

Aurelia nodded solemnly and accepted the heavy book, letting it lie on her legs, which stuck straight out in front of her.

"There's a picture of my mother and father in here." Marian turned the gray pages until she located it. "See?"

Aurelia studied the picture silently.

"There's a picture of me standing in front of my parents' home, too."

Aurelia bent forward to study this likeness closer. "Your hair is different."

Marian grinned. "Yes. Which way do you prefer?"

Aurelia looked from the picture to Marian, then pointed to Marian's head. "This way."

"Good."

Aurelia turned the page to look at the next two pictures, then shifted her gaze back to Marian's. "I wish you weren't going away."

It was all Marian could do to keep the tears from spilling over her bottom lashes. "I do, too, dear, but I'll write you. Won't it be fun to get letters?"

Aurelia only stared at her with wide eyes. "I've never had a letter."

"Well, you shall have more than one by the time I return."

"Can I mail you a letter, too?"

"I should love to receive a letter from you! That is, if your Papa says you may send one."

She watched Aurelia's gaze move high above her shoulder, and knew she was begging her father's approval.

"We'll send her a letter, Aurelia."

We! The word throbbed in her heart.

"Will you really come back, Miss Marian?"

"Yes, I promise. After Christmas, and after New Year's Day, I will be back." She wrinkled her nose playfully, and was rewarded with a small smile. "I don't think I could stay away any longer than that. I'm going to miss you very much."

"I'm going to miss you, too." The words were so low Marian would have missed them if she hadn't been looking at the girl.

"May I have a hug—just a little one—since I'll be missing you so much?"

Marian held her breath. Aurelia stared at her wide-eyed, considering the wisdom of such a move. Had she pushed the girl's new-found camaraderie too far?

Then Aurelia pushed the album from her lap to the divan and scooted forward until her arms barely reached around Marian's neck. With a soft sigh of relief and gratitude, Marian's arms closed lightly around her. A moment later Aurelia's arms grew tighter as she hugged Marian as hard as she could.

It was a long, precious minute before Aurelia released her, and Marian knew she would carry it in her heart forever.

Minutes later Everett helped Marian into a carriage out front, wishing he never had to let go of the hand he took to help her up.

"It wasn't necessary to rent a carriage. I could have hired a cab."

"Mrs. Dorothy preferred I take you to the railroad station."

Truth told, it had been his own idea and funded with his own money. He'd wanted those few minutes alone with her before she left for two weeks.

Two entire weeks! It sounded like eternity with another eternity thrown in for good measure. He'd like to ask her the same thing she'd asked Aurelia: *May I have a hug, since I'll be missing you so much?* As if he'd ever get a wall rebuilt around his heart if he once took her in his arms.

He should be thanking God for the coming two weeks. It would give him time to get his senses back together, shore up that heart of his that felt as full of holes as a sieve.

His throat ached at the picture of his daughter squeezing Marian as though she'd never let go. He'd begun to think Aurelia would never allow herself to care for another young woman. She must be beginning to heal from the scars her mother's abandonment had left.

He cleared his throat. "Thanks for being so good to Aurelia."

He kept his gaze on the blanket covering the horse's back, but he could sense her shoulders relax beneath the heavy cape she wore over her suit, the same suit she had been wearing the day she'd arrived and walked right into his heart.

"She's such a dear child!"

They rode on in silence for three blocks.

"You've been rather touchy this week."

Touchy! He couldn't restrain a broad smile at her prim understatement. She'd done it again. She'd made him smile with the simplest of statements, with looks and words that wouldn't wring a hint of a smile from him for anyone else.

He had been grumpier than usual, he supposed. Since discovering he loved her, he felt as vulnerable around her as a new-born puppy, and it was flat-out uncomfortable.

"Sorry."

They crossed the bridge over the Mississippi within sight of the Falls of St. Anthony, and he thought how that same river ran through River's Edge. The day he met her, she'd stated her preference for travel by steamboat. What would it be like to travel the river with her as man and wife?

Foolish thought!

He asked her plans for her time at home, and drank in the pleasure of listening to her voice until they arrived—all too soon—at the bustling train station.

He arranged for her trunk to be placed in the baggage car, and stayed with her until she was ready to board. "I almost forgot! Can you wait a minute?"

He paused only for assurance she wouldn't board until he returned before sprinting to the carriage and back. He handed her a rectangular package wrapped in mauve paper. "For Christmas, from Aurelia and me."

The pleasure in her face spilled warmth all through him, until he felt like he was out on the Mississippi on a warm summer day instead of standing in the railroad station trying to keep out of the way of a biting north wind.

"I should have thought of it earlier; you could have put it in your trunk." *Did she hug the box slightly closer to her chest?*

"I can take it with me on the car. It's not too large or heavy."

Steam hissed from beneath the wheels nearby, close enough to blow Marian's long navy skirt and expose her high leather shoes, but not close enough to harm them with its heat. The porter clutched the vertical iron railing above the step to the passenger car and reminded Marian it was time to board.

Everett clenched his gloved hands into fists until the muscles hurt. He wanted to pull her into his arms and ask her not to leave so badly he could taste it. He forced himself to keep his face sober while her gaze searched his face, struggled to keep his love for her from showing itself in his eyes.

"Have a blessed Christmas, Everett."

The porter handed her up to the step.

"Marian!"

Almost without realizing it, he was at the step. Her beautiful blue eyes looked into his face, waiting for him to continue just as though there wasn't a train load of people impatient for her to take her seat.

"I. . .I. . .Merry Christmas to you, too."

Her gaze dropped, then lifted to his again immediately. Had some of the light gone out of her eyes? She gave him a tiny smile and disappeared to find her seat.

He watched until the train was out of sight, pushing away the reasonable side of himself that reminded him he'd had no intention of doing any such thing. When he couldn't see even the smallest suggestion of the caboose any longer, he walked slowly back to the carriage, oblivious to the wind whistling around the station and pulling the blanket covering the horse.

If it was this difficult for himself and Aurelia when Marian left for a two-week Christmas trip, what would it be like when she left them for good? Not much chance she'd spend the rest of her life at Aunt Dorothy's. Sooner or later she'd return to her parents' house, or marry that conceited Philander Paget.

The thought should cheer him, considering he was planning to push Marian out of his heart.

nine

Marian lowered herself to the worn wooden chair opposite Sheriff Tucker's desk and unobtrusively flexed her gloved fingers. She'd been clenching her reticule so tightly her hands were cramped. The muscles in her face must be tight also, for her head felt as though it were caught tight in one of the vises in Everett's woodworking room at the mission.

The thought of Everett wasn't relaxing. What would he think if he knew of this visit to the Rivers' Edge Prison to see an accused thief, a man who had kidnapped her, a man to whom she'd been engaged?

Sheriff Tucker squeezed his round body into his chair with a grunt that twitched his red handlebar mustache. "It's surprised I am to see you here, Miss Ames. What might I be doing for you?"

"I came to visit Rasmus Pierce." Actually, her heart was beating a mile a minute with the fear she might see Rasmus, but she was certain it was what God wished.

"Ah." Sheriff Tucker tented his fat fingers and puffed out a loud sigh. "You sure you're wanting to do that? He isn't a right gentlemanly type."

"I know what manner of man Mr. Pierce is." She continued to meet his gaze in spite of the warmth rising over her neck and face. He'd evidently forgotten momentarily that she'd been engaged to Rasmus.

"I guess you do at that." With difficulty, he pushed himself out of the chair. "All four cells are full, mainly with Rasmus and his gang. S'pose you'd just as soon have a bit of privacy for your talk."

"Please."

"Right." He indicated a rectangular oak library table at one side of the room. "You can talk there. I'll bring him out." He hesitated a moment. "I should be warning you, lass. He's been a right rowdy prisoner, so I've had to keep him in cuffs often. They've torn his wrists up a mite."

He stopped at a heavy closed door she suspected led to the cells. "If you were my daughter, I wouldn't be allowing you to visit prisoners the likes of Pierce."

"I dare say my father would agree with your sentiments, but I am of age."

"Yes," he mumbled through his huge mustache, "more's the pity."

She'd rather not be here herself, but she believed God was prodding her to visit Rasmus. She moved to the oak table, asking the Lord to calm her and bring to mind what she should say.

A moment later, Rasmus walked into the room in front of Sheriff Tucker. His faded red and cream flannel shirt and worn brown corduroys were wrinkled. His black hair had grown considerably since she'd last seen him. It hung straight and stringy over his frayed collar. A thin mustache accentuated his narrow face.

Mostly she noticed the handcuffs on his bandaged wrists, and stifled a shocked gasp.

"Hello, Rasmus."

She could see in his eyes the unpleasant shock her identity caused. His angry gaze shifted to Sheriff Tucker. "Take me back to my cell."

Marian started, one arm reaching toward him, though he was six feet away from her. "*Please,* Rasmus!"

He stopped, his back as straight and rigid as the prison walls. The sheriff waited, watching him.

She knew when Rasmus gave in by the barely noticeable

shift in his shoulders.

He turned and walked the short distance to the table, sitting down opposite her, still not looking at her.

She was embarrassed for him. She knew he wouldn't have wanted her to see him with his hands in cuffs. She wished the sheriff would at least allow him the dignity of having his hands free, but she was afraid to ask it for fear the request would be denied, and Rasmus' embarrassment increased.

The sheriff moved to his desk. Marian was grateful for his thoughtfulness in giving them as much privacy as possible in the small space.

Now that she was here, she didn't know how to begin. She glanced down at her lap and ran her tongue along her lips, which felt parched. When she looked back up, Rasmus was finally looking at her. She caught the longing in his eyes before he tried to cover it with indifference.

Her glance shifted as she sought for words, and landed on his cuffed wrists.

His hands slipped from the table to his lap, and she knew he'd seen her notice the cuffs.

"You have only fifteen minutes," the sheriff reminded them.

Marian took a deep breath and forced herself to look directly into Rasmus' eyes. It was only fair to do so, when she'd forced him into the embarrassing position of seeing his former fiancée in his present condition.

"Why did ya come, Marian?"

The words were stiff, but with anger or embarrassment, she couldn't tell. His eyes were almost black, and she wondered what kind of wounds he had inside, in his heart and emotions. Were they as bad as the wounds on his wrists?

"I. . .I wanted to tell you I forgive you."

As soon as the words were out she wanted to snatch them back. They were true, but they sounded so pompous.

Hands still in his lap, he leaned forward, his eyes mere slits.

"Forgive me fer what? Lovin' ya?"

It was difficult to keep looking at him. "No. For kidnapping me and Justin's nephew and niece."

He turned his face away, but looked back in a second, and she wondered if the sheriff had heard his ragged, indrawn breath.

"I was wrong to snatch ya thet way, and I'm sorry." His voice was low, and she knew he didn't want Sheriff Tucker to hear him admit to a woman he'd committed a wrongdoing. "But, Marian, I loved ya so! I figgered if I could jest git ya away with me fer awhile, ya'd learn ta love me, too."

"I. . .I need to ask your forgiveness, also."

Surprise set him against the back of the chair so suddenly he almost tipped over. "What fer?"

"I was wrong to accept your marriage proposal. I agreed to marry you for the wrong reason."

She noticed his teeth clench, and winced.

"Ya mean ya wanted ta git back at Justin Knight fer marryin' someone else."

"Yes." Now she was the one wishing there was no one else to hear their conversation.

One side of his mouth slipped into a sarcastic smile. "So ya want ta fergive me fer takin' you and the kids by force. Don't want ta fergive me fer makin' Justin marry that other female?"

Heat spread over her face. "Well, not exactly. You probably did me a favor. I discovered I didn't love Justin. Not that it was acceptable for you to arrange a shotgun wedding for him!" she added vehemently.

"So ya don't love Justin."

She shifted uncomfortably. "I didn't come here to speak of the state of my heart."

"Somethin' more ya want ta fergive me fer thet ya haven't mentioned?" he challenged.

"No. I wanted to tell you that through all that happened—

Justin's marriage, and being held captive at your hideout and all—I learned a lot about myself, and I didn't like what I saw. I realized I spent all my energy trying to please myself."

He scowled. "What's wrong with thet?"

"Everything. After all that happened, I told God I wanted to start living to please Him."

She wouldn't have believed his hard, almost black eyes could be so tender. A real smile spread across his thin face. "Marian, yer jest about the most innocent thing I ever saw. Why, you've got no more bad ways in ya than a. . .a butterfly has. What could ya hev ever done ta make God anythin' but pleased?"

"Live for myself rather than for others, as Christ lived His life for us." She glanced quickly down at her lap and back up again. "Not that I never have selfish wishes any longer, but since I turned my life over to God, He's been changing me."

Rasmus shook his head, and Marian almost lost hope at the amusement on his face. "Never thought ya'd turn religious on me."

"It's a good thing, Rasmus, learning about God and the ways He wishes people to live. I wanted to tell you about my experience because, well, because I want you to have the peace and contentment I've found."

His eyebrows shifted up like two pointed parentheses. "Kin ya see me playin' a religious man?"

"I can see you living as a man who loves God, yes."

His gaze searched hers, and she wondered if he was trying to figure out whether she was serious.

"God wouldn't want the likes of me usin' His name."

"If you recall some of the stories from the Bible, there's a lot of men who did things far worse than you who changed their ways and began using His name, and He never claimed any of them shouldn't do so. Once a man starts walking with God, God doesn't walk away from him."

She could see his discomfort in his shifting gaze. "Never

had much use fer the Bible," he muttered.

"Only two minutes left."

She almost jumped at the sheriff's reminder. She'd become so intensely involved in their discussion that she'd forgotten he was in the room.

"Oh, there was so much more I wished to say."

"Ya know, yer the only one 'sides Ma and Pa thet hev come ta visit me."

She could tell it was hard for him to admit that.

"Would ya consider writin' ta me?"

She hadn't thought it would come to this. She'd only planned to visit him, urge him to follow the Lord, and leave with her duty done.

"I'll write if you wish, but I shan't mislead you into thinking the letters mean. . .that I care for you. I shan't become engaged to you again."

He rested his forearms on the table and leaned forward, his voice low and urgent. "I love ya, Marian. I've loved ya fer years. I wouldn't be here now if I didn't love ya so much. The law couldn't git close ta me in Missouri. The only reason I came back ta Minnesota was ta keep Justin Knight from marryin' ya. The only reason the Pinkerton detectives caught me, is 'cause I was so crazy 'bout ya I lost all sense."

"I'm sorry." She could barely hear her own whisper. His words shamed her. No matter that he was a criminal, that he'd robbed, kidnapped, even wounded some people. His sins didn't excuse her for using his love as a means of revenge against another.

"Yeah, me too. Guess we did quite a job of hurtin' each other. But I'd still be mighty glad ta receive yer letters."

Would her letters give him the strength to reform? "I'll write."

He winked at her, and a smile almost like his confident old one slid across his face. "Then I'll be good as gold 'round here."

The sheriff started toward them. "Time's up."

She stood when Rasmus stood. "Wait, please." She pulled a small black leather Bible from her handbag and held it toward Rasmus. "I'd like you to have this."

He stared at her, and she wondered whether he wanted to say no, but didn't wish to hurt her feelings at the end of their interview. She tried not to stare at the handcuffs when he took the book from her.

"I hope you'll read it."

He hesitated once more. "I'll think on it."

Sheriff Tucker touched his arm. "Come on, Pierce."

Rasmus gave her one sharp nod over his shoulder. "I'll be thinkin' on what ya said, too."

When Sheriff Tucker returned, he settled fat hands on his wide hips, puffing, and regarded her over his huge mustache. "Are you all right?"

She didn't realize until that moment that she was trembling.

"I'm fine. Fifteen minutes is such a short time." She flushed. "That sounds as though I'm ungrateful to you for arranging our meeting. I'm not, but I couldn't think of everything I wanted to say. I'm afraid I didn't say the right things to convince him to turn to God."

"Miss Ames, about that Bible and all. . .A prison atmosphere seldom encourages a man to become religious. If a prisoner does have a change of heart, it takes a great deal of courage to make it known. Keep hoping for him if you must, but don't look for him to be talking much about it."

ten

Everett entered the kitchen, glad to leave behind the cutting January wind. The cold seemed more bitter than usual this year, though the temperatures were milder than normal. Maybe he was getting old. Twenty-six didn't sound old, but he felt down-right ancient.

He pulled off his snow-encrusted gloves and massaged his eyes wearily with a thumb and forefinger. Might as well be honest with himself; not only the weather but life itself seemed cold since Marian had left for River's Edge. No word yet when she'd return.

He'd known it would be tough pushing her back out of his heart, but he'd badly underestimated just how tough. *About like a makeshift wooden fence trying to hold back the Mississippi during a raging flood,* he thought wryly, starting to unbutton his jacket.

A whisper of sound brought his attention to the swinging hallway door. His hands stopped in the midst of freeing a button. "Marian, you're home!"

Her wonderful smile broke across her delicate face like the sun breaking across a still Minnesota lake on a clear morning. "Yes, I'm home."

His heart leaped to life. *Traitor,* he accused it silently, bending over to remove his thick boots. The action took far longer than necessary while he strove to avoid meeting her gaze. In spite of how much he'd missed her, he'd resolved he would absolutely rebuild a wall of reserve and indifference between them, even if he had to be rude to be successful. Then the first time he saw her, he grinned like the Cheshire cat. Even now, looking at his stupid Alaskas instead of her beautiful face, he couldn't stop smiling.

It was just that she'd taken him by surprise again. She was always doing that. Even the first time they'd met, he'd looked into her blue eyes, heard her silvery laugh, and before he'd known what was happening he'd responded to her like an abandoned puppy who'd just found a home.

He knew she was still in the room. He could feel her presence. "So how was River's Edge?"

He straightened, turning to face the wall to remove his muffler, hat, and coat. He moved slowly, making the actions last as long as possible. Maybe by the time he had his things hanging on the wooden pegs beside the door he'd manage to ditch this stupid smile and put on the mask he intended to wear around her.

"It was nice to see Mother and Father again, but I'm glad to be back. I was lonely."

Her last words froze his hands on his jacket. *Lonely for him? Stupid hope. As if a lady of Marian's upbringing would say such a thing to a man who wasn't courting her.* He slipped on the shoes he'd left beside the door. "Missed all those kindergarten kids, I suppose."

"Yes. I hadn't realized how attached I've grown to the children, and everyone else I've come to know here the last couple months."

He swallowed hard, bit his lips to try once more to get some control over that out-of-hand smile. Convinced he'd succeeded, he turned around.

Adversely, he was disappointed to find her back to him while she poured a glass of water.

She turned, smiling at him again, and before he could stop himself, he was smiling back. He decided to pour himself a glass of water, too, so he'd be forced to look at something besides her.

It was a mistake. She was still standing beside the iron sink, and her nearness set every nerve ending in his body pulsating. The lilac fragrance she wore wrapped around him like a warm spring day.

"Thank you for the wooden box you and Aurelia gave me for Christmas."

He leaned back against the cold iron of the sink and played with the glass in his hand, watching the water tilt in small waves. He'd given her the box she'd admired the first day she had come to the woodworking shop, saying it was from both himself and Aurelia, because it seemed too personal a gift for a woman with whom he wasn't actively pursuing a relationship.

He'd wondered every day what she'd thought of it, imagined her rubbing her soft, tiny fingers with their buffed nails over the top, admiring his work the way she had in the shop.

Now he only shrugged. "It was just a box."

"I like it, just the same."

Her voice was uncharacteristically quiet and low with disappointment, and he couldn't keep himself from glancing at her. The usual light in her eyes was dimmed, and the realization was like a sudden wound to his chest. He was sorely tempted to take back his indifferent remark, but it was better like this. It was what he'd intended all along—to treat her as though she and anything concerning her weren't important to him.

But he hadn't expected her eyes to look like bruised flower petals after a hard rain.

He took a deep breath and buried his frustration. "A town in South Dakota sent Mayor Eustis seven hundred and fifty pounds of jackrabbits for the next charity baskets, which are to be delivered in a couple weeks."

"Jackrabbits!" It brought the laugh he'd hoped it would. The sound was sweet, filling the kitchen and warming his soul. He'd missed her laugh these last two weeks.

The kitchen door swung open, letting in a rush of chilling

winter wind, along with Mrs. Dorothy, Sonja, and Aurelia.

In a moment the three of them were all over Marian, laughing and talking all at once. He noticed, though, that she gave most of her attention to Aurelia, who leaned happily against her leg, beaming up at her. She hadn't removed her snow-covered outer garments, but Marian didn't object, though he could see her rust-colored wool gown was damp.

Marian's arm rested on the girl's shoulder, keeping her close. "I've missed all of you," she said, but she was looking at Aurelia when she said it, and an aching lump settled in Everett's chest.

Sonja nodded, her smile large. "*Ja. Mormor* alvays says, 'Being avay is fine, but being at home is best.'"

"Yes," Marian agreed. "Being at home is best."

Does she really think of this as her home now? he wondered.

Aurelia tugged at Marian's hand. "Come see what Papa gave me for Christmas!"

Everett landed a hand on her shoulder. "Whoa, there. Let's take off your coat and boots first. As it is, Sonja will have to clean up the kitchen floor."

Sonja and Dorothy looked down at their feet in surprise, and Sonja's hearty laugh burst forth. "*Uff da!* Ve forgot the snow for seeing Miss Marian!"

Aurelia removed her winter protection in record time, and pulled Marian toward her room, calling over her shoulder, "You come, too, Papa!"

What could he do but follow, he argued with the part of his brain that admonished him to stay away from Marian.

Aurelia's room, which was beside his own on the second floor, was the destination. As always when he entered, warm pleasure filled him at the simple beauty. Dorothy had insisted on redoing the room for Aurelia when he and the girl had moved into the house. Her action in welcoming his daughter had won his loyalty forever.

Wallpaper with a simple design of pink rosebuds on a white background were perfect for a small girl's room. White lace curtains hung at the long windows. A small desk was draped in white lace caught up in large pink bows, and a mirror in a pretty cast-iron stand stood on top.

But it was the small cupboard he'd made for her as a Christmas gift that was the object of Aurelia's attention at the moment. He leaned a shoulder against the door frame, hooking his thumbs in the pockets of his flannel trousers, and watched the excitement on his daughter's face as she showed off his gift.

Marian slid her fingers over the curving lines of the cupboard that wasn't quite as tall as she was herself, and Everett's ego swelled in spite of himself at the open admiration in her eyes.

He hadn't done such a bad job on it, if he did say so himself. Shelves on top held Aurelia's few books and some of the things she'd made at kindergarten: a clay duck (or so she claimed), a piece of cardboard with a design of a pine tree stitched with thick green shoelace, a basket unevenly woven from blue and yellow paper. Behind the doors in the bottom half, Aurelia stored her toys. The bright white paint made the piece fit well with the room.

"Papa made it. Isn't it beautiful?"

"Very beautiful. Look at the flowers he painted on the doors and along the top, Aurelia! They match the pink roses on your wallpaper." She reached a slender finger to gently touch one of the flowers.

She turned awe-filled eyes in his direction, and he shifted his feet uncomfortably. "It's lovely, Everett. The entire cupboard is lovely. When did you ever find time to make it?"

"I worked on it in spare minutes between other projects at the workshop. Remember telling me a child needs a place to display the things she makes in kindergarten?"

Aurelia tugged at her arm. "We hung the picture you gave us over there." She pointed at a spot on the wall opposite her bed. "It's my favorite picture."

Everett followed them across the room. Marian properly admired the small framed print of Minnehaha Falls, telling Aurelia she'd placed it in the perfect spot.

"She wanted it where she could see it when she woke up in the morning," he said softly from behind her. When she turned around, they were only inches apart, and he retreated a step, trying not to appear as though he was running away. "It was the perfect Christmas gift. We both love it."

Her eyes lit up at his words, and the smile in them lit up his heart again.

A short, plump, dark-haired girl wearing the black dress and white apron of a maid bustled past the doorway, and Marian stared in surprise.

"That's Anna," he explained. "Mrs. Dorothy hired her to help Sonja with the housework. She said Sonja had more than she could properly manage. I suspect the more complete truth is that Mrs. Dorothy's decided to help the unemployment situation out a bit herself."

Marian grinned. "That would be like her, wouldn't it?"

He rammed his hands in his back pockets. "Well, I'd better be checking with Mrs. Dorothy. She said there's a shutter she'd like me to tighten before dark."

He wasn't doing too well with his resolve to keep Marian at arm's length from his heart, he thought, making his way downstairs. He wasn't so sure he wanted to fight his attraction to her any longer, even though he knew nothing could ever come of it. Just those few minutes with her had made him feel human again for the first time since she'd left. Even his heart felt like it smiled when she was around.

He slowed when he reached the bottom step, cinching his elbow around the balustrade's large round peak. When Marian was around, sweetness and joy rested his spirit.

Which was dangerous. He longed to believe she could be faithful in love, that her enjoyment of the exciting social life and beautiful things money can buy wouldn't keep her from committing herself completely and happily to a man of modest means and entertainments such as himself.

"You are dull as dishwater, Everett Starr. Dull and poor, and you'll never be anything else. I can't imagine why I ever agreed to marry you."

His wife's words rang through his brain for the thousandth time, and his jaw began to throb from his clenched teeth. That accusation had been part of a long speech she'd flung at him, mostly in a high-pitched scream, the night she'd left. If it hadn't been for Aurelia, he didn't know how he would have survived the next few months and years. His daughter gave him something to live for, her future gave him something to look forward to and struggle toward.

He moved his jaw slowly back and forth, lessening the tension in his face, and slowly unclenched his hands, straightening his stiff fingers. He might be hopelessly and eternally in love with Marian, but he wasn't about to tell her. He wasn't going to be fool enough to ask for a commitment from her, and put his heart on the chopping block again. Nothing on the face of the earth was worth taking that risk.

eleven

To Everett's satisfaction, Minneapolis' citizens were shocked at the extent of poverty revealed by the mayor's Christmas basket campaign, and drew together like one great family to meet the needs with cheerful resolve.

Invitations arrived daily for Marian and Dorothy. Every social event of the season was "for sweet charity," and Marian attended a number of them with Philander Paget.

After the city's Associated Charities announced it had given over ten thousand pieces of clothing away, and the need was still great, the Kindergarten and Industrial Association received more donations of used clothing than ever before. When the church's usual needlework volunteers could not keep up with the mending necessary for the donations, Dorothy and Marian held a Thimble Bee at the house. The downstairs overflowed with women and young ladies diligently stitching away while listening to the parlor readings and music Dorothy provided. Sonja and Anna were joined by two young women hired for the day, and provided delightfully delicate sandwiches and cakes for the workers.

Mrs. Turner, the mission greeter, arrived with a bevy of her neighbor women in hand. Marian discovered the taciturn woman had been involved for years in the local Needlework Guild, which supplied new and used garments to local charities, supplying over 4,500 garments in the past year alone. Marian's estimation of the woman took a large leap forward, and she determined to judge people less quickly in the future.

The day after the Thimble Bee, Dorothy decided the parlor, dining room, and hall simply *must* have new wallpaper, and the household members' lives were turned topsy-turvy for weeks while two unemployed, married men removed and replaced the wallcoverings. Marian thought the new cream silk walls with rose and gold borders furnished a lovely background for the rose-silk and brocade furniture, but she suspected the furnishings were no more necessary than Anna's services.

Local sawmills donated wood when it was discovered families needed fuel as much as food. Sonja's married brother lent his wagon and team, and Everett hired two unemployed men to drive the team for deliveries.

When the mayor announced the city would be purchasing flour wholesale for the police cook to make into bread to supplement the daily free soup, Mrs. Turner came up with a bread plan for the mission. Mission volunteers brought loaves of bread daily and left them on an unattended table outside the room for donated clothing. News of its existence soon became known by word of mouth. The bread was free to all who needed it, and any who would like to contribute were welcome to leave a loaf. Every morning the table was covered with bread. Every evening the table was bare.

Sonja and Anna made extra loaves each baking day for the mission table and to have available for the many men who stopped daily at the back doors across the city asking whether there were chores for day laborers.

By the mayor's second basket delivery in mid-January, the city's estimate of unemployed increased substantially. Almost one thousand families received baskets this time. Mayor Eustis decided a family could not exist on a basket a month, and from that point on, patrol wagons were sent on daily bread routes, the police assisted by unemployed men.

It was discovered Hennepin County in Minneapolis had the highest number of paupers in the state, and the highest unemployment was in the sixth ward of the county, where the mission stood.

On every street corner, in every business establishment, in sermons, in thimble-bees, wherever people met, the topic was the "worthy" versus the "unworthy" poor. Many felt only the severest cases should receive assistance, and only those who were destitute for reasons totally beyond their control were considered worthy. "The lazy and the servant of alcohol or gambling dens need not apply" was their motto, followed closely by "Careless and indiscriminate giving does more harm than good since it encourages idleness." Philander Paget repeated the mottos on every opportunity.

Personally, Marian hadn't met anyone who enjoyed begging. She was concerned that the city charities determined worthiness by the head of the household.

"Should a wife and children go hungry and cold because of the husband and father's weakness?" she argued whenever the topic arose.

She did not keep silent on her views at social engagements, and Philander more than once accused her of embarrassing him, and speaking of things beyond her ken. However, many of the businessmen and politicians, hearing her argument, went away reflecting on her comments.

Marian noted the contributions Dorothy and Everett were making in supplying work for the unemployed, and wished there was a more direct manner in which she could assist. Giving money was easy, but she heard often that the unemployed preferred performing paying work to receiving charity. Not owning a house, she couldn't hire workmen or domestic help.

After a struggle with herself, she hired a seamstress to make a few simple gowns. She didn't truly need more clothes, but she could easily afford them, and it provided income to the seamstress, whose husband and oldest son were out of work.

When she received an invitation to Mrs. Thomas Lowry's Birthday Bag charity event, she requested the seamstress to remake one of her best trousseau pieces to better fit the season's fashions. There wasn't time to make an entire gown, and this would be one of *the* social events of the season. After all, Mrs. Lowry of Lowry Hill was the wife of one of Minneapolis' primary businessmen, President of the Twin-City Rapid Transit Company which ran the electric trolleys.

Everett was loud in his disapproval of the event, which was eagerly discussed in the newspapers in advance of the date.

"Typical of society's idea of charity; attend an afternoon social with a bag of pennies and think they are helping the unemployed."

Marian's fingers tightened on her needle, but she said nothing. Guilt seeped over the contentment she'd felt while sewing buttons onto coats donated to the mission. She and Philander were planning to attend the social, and not once had it occurred to her that they were selfish to do so.

Dorothy looked up from the brown wool jacket she was mending to respond mildly, "Granted, the silk bags each guest will fill with a penny for each year of her life won't provide a lot of money. The bags were sent with the invitations as an added incentive to attend."

"As if any social butterfly would need inducement to attend an event at the Lowry mansion."

Marian couldn't deny the truth of his statement. She'd already heard a number of girls exclaiming over the opportunity to view the fine home.

Dorothy attended to her mending, but continued placatingly, "A number of entertainments will be scattered throughout the house, and guests will pay for each element they choose to enjoy, thereby raising more funds."

Everett tossed the paper aside in crackling disarray. "*One* of the expensive new gowns the socialites purchase for the event could easily feed an unemployed man's family for months."

"Ouch!"

Marian's needle lodged in her thumb and tears sprang to her eyes. She jerked the offending item out and rose trembling, the garment falling unheeded at her feet.

"Must you always be so. . .so discouraging? Must you always look only at what isn't being accomplished and how much more needs to be done? Must you always belittle what aid is given?" She clutched her throbbing thumb, the sight of the spot of blood adding to her fury. "Do you think you are the only person who gives from a pure heart? Just *once,*" she stamped to the door, shaking her hand furiously, "just once I should like to hear you praise another's efforts."

She rushed toward the kitchen, her heart thumping wildly. She didn't understand the man at all. He was a patient and loving father. His devotion to the mission and the Newsboys was heartwarming. He cared deeply for his neighbors and community. Why, *why* was he so bitter? Surely losing his wife couldn't account for the anger he had toward the entire world.

She dabbed at her thumb with a wet cloth. Above all, she wanted Everett's heart healed. Whenever he lashed out at the world as he had this afternoon, she wanted to comfort him. The knowledge she hadn't that right frustrated her. That was the true reason she'd exploded at him in the parlor like a box of firecrackers all set off at once, she admitted to herself.

"Please, heal him, Lord." She'd repeated that prayer often since meeting Everett. Would she ever see it answered?

A familiar "whoosh" sent a wave of despair over her. Someone had entered the kitchen through the swinging door. Her tirade had left her too exhausted to speak with anyone. She'd make an excuse and leave.

A decidedly masculine throat clearing froze her in place.

"Marian?"

She turned about slowly. Everett's brown eyes were filled with apology and misery.

"I'm sorry."

They spoke it together. Small smiles worked at their tense lips.

One of Everett's hands rubbed the back of his neck. "Afraid

I acted the fool once more."

"No, I—"

"Yes. Decidedly yes. Mrs. Dorothy explained that the women attending the social affairs give employment to seamstresses and store clerks and milliners, that the hosts and hostesses hire musicians and domestics, purchase food and flowers." His broad shoulders lifted his white, collarless cotton shirt in a shrug. "I'd never thought of it that way. Truce?"

Smiling, she held out a hand.

He took it immediately, keeping hold of it after he shook it, looking down into her eyes from only a foot away until she could barely breathe from her notice of his touch.

"I'm sorry I yelled at you."

His fingers squeezed hers more tightly and her heart spun. "You didn't yell. Raised your voice, a little." His grin was wonderful. "I wouldn't have been surprised if you'd thrown something at me."

She jerked her hand from his as if burned. The memory of herself throwing the porcelain figurine at Justin when he had told her of his marriage to Constance flashed across her mind. Had Everett somehow heard of it? Of course not. How could he? She'd been too ashamed of her actions to tell anyone.

Everett took a step backward, consternation in every line of his face. "Now I've insulted you. I meant it as a joke."

"I'm afraid my temper is not my best point. Anyway, I wasn't angry with you when I displayed it earlier, it was just that—" she paused. "Never mind."

His brow puzzled. "What is it?"

"I just hate to see you so angry with the world."

The friendly eyes became suddenly flint hard. "The world isn't a fair place."

"No, it's not. It isn't about to change because you or I wish it to do so. Doesn't that mean we should be all the more grateful for those people who love justice and fair play, and follow the

Lord's command to love one another?"

"And ignore the injustices and the people who are hurt and needy?"

"Of course not ignore them. Be glad for others who don't ignore them, even if they try to meet the needs in manners other than ours."

Skepticism filled his face, and she sighed, feeling more exhausted than ever.

Sonja and Anna bustled into the room, greeting them with smiles and chatter, and Everett excused himself stiffly.

Marian tried to carry on a conversation with the maids, but she couldn't keep her mind from Everett. Had she stumbled in and tried to fix something she should have left to the Lord? Would her actions push Everett further from her, and build his walls of bitterness higher?

❧

Marian helped a boy with unruly mud-brown hair, an overabundance of energy, and an amazing lack of motor skills wield the small, dull scissors around the tip of the red paper heart. "There, Erik! Now it's all ready to glue to the white piece of paper, and your mother's valentine will be done."

In one motion, he pushed back his chair and stood, reaching in front of the quiet blond girl beside him to get the jar of white paste. "Do you think *Mor* will like it, teacher?"

She loved hearing the term "teacher" on the children's lips, though technically she was still only an assistant to Jessie Watkins. "She'll love it, Erik."

Fingers linked lightly behind her, she strolled around the table of five-year-olds who were her responsibility this afternoon, complimenting and encouraging their creative attempts, helping with a torn heart here, a crooked heart there.

Aurelia sat at the end of one of the low, rectangular wooden tables, bent over work, a thick red crayon clutched in one hand, her almost-invisible blond brows drawn together in concentration. Right before Marian reached her, Aurelia straightened and sat back in her chair, studying her work.

Marian knelt beside her. "Is this valentine for your father?"

She nodded soberly.

"May I see?"

Aurelia nodded again, and Marian picked up the heavy white piece of paper. The girl hadn't chosen to make a red paper heart, as had most of the children. Instead she'd drawn two stick figures with wobbly, egg-shaped torsos. On each figure's body she'd drawn a big red heart with her crayon, and filled it in with color. The taller figure had little red circles trailing from its heart to its feet.

Hardly a cheerful picture, she thought in alarm.

"Is this you and your father?"

"Yes." Aurelia pointed to the figure with the trailing circles. "That's Papa."

Marian's fingertip traced the trail of red circles. "What are these spots?"

"Tears."

"Why?"

"Because ever since Mama left us, Papa's heart has been sad."

Marian thought her own heart would start crying at the child's straightforward, unemotional explanation. Was that why she was such a timid, hesitant-to-trust child? Was it sadness for her father that made her that way? How many children were sensitive enough to sense their parents' pain?

She hated to think of the pain this would bring to him.

"Maybe together we can think up a valentine that will make his heart happy."

Aurelia's little blond brows lifted in question. "Like what?"

Marian rested an index finger on her bottom lip as if concentrating. "What do you think he likes better than anything else in the world?"

"Pound cake."

The instant, confident reply tripped a laugh that released some of the tension in Marian's chest. "He definitely likes pound cake, but there's something he likes more than that."

"What?"

Marian bounced her index finger lightly off Aurelia's nose. "You. There is nothing that makes your father happier than you."

Aurelia stared at her, her eyes growing wide with wonder at the thought. A smile started and spread slowly until it filled her face. "Me?"

Marian nodded. "Absolutely, positively. Maybe you could draw your father a heart with a picture of you inside it. That would be like putting the thing that makes him happiest inside his heart."

"He would be happy then, wouldn't he?"

Marian smoothed the fine blond hair unnecessarily. "Your love for him gives him great happiness, dear. If you'd like, we can ask Sonja to bake him a pound cake, too."

"Oh, yes! Let's!"

When Aurelia was busy with her new drawing, Marian slipped the first attempt away from the table, rolling it discreetly while giving her attention to her other charges.

That evening Aurelia could hardly wait for dinner to be over before giving the drawing to her father, but she decided herself to wait until they'd had the pound cake Sonja had already prepared for dessert. When she presented her valentine, she explained carefully to her father that she was the figure inside his heart. He hugged her close with one arm, his cheek resting against her fine blond hair, and told her he loved the drawing.

Marian was sure the sheen she saw in his eyes before he bent his head over his daughter were tears, and her throat grew thick with the memory of Aurelia's first picture, and what it would have done to this dear man.

She wished she hadn't agreed to join Philander and a group of their favorite friends on a sleighing party this evening. She would have preferred to spend the time with Dorothy, Everett, and Aurelia. They'd grown so dear to her, and she enjoyed the sweet peace of their home-times together.

Philander had sent her a valentine in the mail. The gilt-edged red heart with a grinning red-satin cupid lay open on the small inlaid hall table, the verse by Sherman plainly revealed to the world:

> *Day to my heart*
> *With you comes always fair,*
> *When you depart*
> *'Tis twilight there.*

She passed by it, its presence forgotten, when she went to dress for the sleighing party.

But Everett noticed it later, and hated the words that tied Philander Paget to the woman Everett loved.

Sonja passed by while he was at the table. Embarrassed to be caught reading Marian's love note, he grinned awkwardly. "Did you receive any valentines from your beaus, Sonja?"

"*Uff da!* Not a vun." A large sigh lifted her shoulders and she shook her head. "*Mormor* says, 'A life without luff is like a year without summer.' I am ready for summer!"

Everett silently but heartily agreed.

&

Do I dare show him Aurelia's valentine? Marian looked at the piece of paper lying on her bureau, the edges curling.

She'd worried over it all week, hating the thought of the pain it would bring Everett, yet wondering whether he hadn't the right to know what his daughter thought she saw in him. In church this morning she thought she'd finally come to a decision. Now that she had the opportunity to tell him, she was questioning her decision.

"You're just being a chicken-heart," she accused herself. "You don't want to be the one to bring him any pain, even if it's best for Aurelia."

With sudden determination, she grabbed the paper and hurried out of the room before she could change her mind again.

She found Everett where she expected, in the overstuffed chair in the corner of the parlor, poring over the Sunday edition of the *Minneapolis Tribune*. For a change, he was alone in the room.

He glanced up while she hesitated in the doorway, as though he'd sensed her presence. A warm glow heated his glance before the all-too-familiar shade dropped over his eyes. The "no trespassing" message she read there was discouraging, but for Aurelia's sake she gripped her courage and went to stand beside his chair.

He lowered the newspaper slowly, watching her with something akin to alarm behind his guarded expression. She knew he was wondering why she was approaching him in such an uncharacteristic manner, and her face flushed uncomfortably. Her gaze dropped from his a moment in an attempt to regain her composure, and she noticed he'd been reading the weekly society page.

The fact side-tracked her momentarily. She wouldn't have thought him a man who bothered about society's parties, who was visiting whom, the latest tilt a lady should have to her hat, or newest manner for a man to wear his tie.

She didn't try to keep the laughter from the questioning glance she flashed at him.

He folded the paper in quarters quickly and noisily, and dropped it at his feet. "There was a piece about the sleighing party you were with Valentine's evening."

His voice was gruff with embarrassment.

It only increased her amusement. "Oh." She was tempted to

use this weapon to the fullest and tease him unmercifully, but there was Aurelia's valentine to consider.

The picture was almost burning her hands. She stared down at it, trying to work up the courage to show it to him, hating that she was the only one who could tell him of this aspect of his daughter's love.

"What is it, Marian? Is something wrong?"

How could she tell him what Aurelia had said?

His large, rough hand touched hers, his fingers closing over the edge of the thick paper. "Is it something to do with this?"

She took a deep breath, lifting her chin to look squarely into his eyes. If she was going to hurt him, she wouldn't shrink behind a cowardly manner. "Before Aurelia drew the valentine she gave you, she made you this."

Reluctantly, she released it.

A scowl puzzled his brow, drawing his thick, dark eyebrows together. His gaze darted back to her, and she saw the confusion in his eyes. He waited silently for her explanation.

The fingertips of one hand played restlessly with the nails of the other. "It's a picture of you and Aurelia. You're the one with the crying heart."

He dropped his attention back to the picture, and she lowered herself to the large upholstered hassock in front of his chair.

His scowl deepened. "Crying?"

She nodded. "Aurelia said your heart is always sad."

One oversized hand swung out, palm up, in a gesture of frustration, and he shook his head in disbelief. "Why would she say that?"

Reluctantly, she relayed Aurelia's explanation. The pain in his face lanced right through her. It must be difficult enough for him to hear of the sadness his daughter felt for him; to have someone else not only know of it but inform him of it must increase his discomfort.

She shifted slightly on the hassock, resisting the temptation to study her fingernails to avoid his eyes. "I've been arguing with myself for days over whether to show this to you. I decided if I were a parent, I would want to know if my child felt this way."

He nodded briskly. Quickly rolling the paper up, he propped his elbows on the fat, overstuffed plush arms of the chair and rested his forehead on his clasped hands, which clutched the paper roll.

The pain filling the silence was overwhelming. Marian longed to put her arms around his broad shoulders and comfort him, but all she could do was whisper a prayer for him while she left the room.

twelve

Marian dabbed the tears from her eyes before answering the knock on her bedroom door fifteen minutes later. She didn't want Aunt Dorothy to see the evidence of her little sob-fest.

A glance in the mirror convinced her that just wiping the tears away wasn't enough to fool anyone.

"One minute, please," she called.

Shakily, she poured a bit of water from the rose-decorated ivory pitcher into the matching bowl and splashed her face. Patting it dry, she chanced another hopeful glance in the long mirror. *Better, but not perfect.*

She drew a ragged little breath and opened the door.

Aunt Dorothy wasn't there. Instead, Everett stood with his hands jammed into the pockets of his best Sunday gray worsted slacks with the blue stripes, his face looking as worn as a piece of driftwood tossed up by the Mississippi and weathered for a hundred years on a sun-drenched bank.

He cleared his throat, but his voice was still rough when he spoke. "I'm going to Minnehaha Falls. I thought. . .that is, I wondered. . .Will you come?" he ended in a rush.

She nodded, too shocked at his invitation to find her voice. She couldn't imagine what had possessed him to visit the falls in the middle of winter, but if he wanted her company there or anywhere else, she would move mountains to accompany him.

"Better dress warm. And wear boots. The snow might not be cleared from the paths."

They took the Minnehaha Line trolley. Everett was silent the entire trip, watching the white landscape flash past the windows. Marian tried not to stare at him, and almost bit her tongue through in her struggle not to urge him to share his thoughts. Aunt Dorothy had agreed to watch Aurelia for the afternoon, and for Marian it was enough for now that Everett wanted her alone with him in his pain.

She lifted a silent prayer for the Lord's comfort for Everett, and wisdom for herself. She generally gave her opinion whether or not it was desired, and without much thought. Everett didn't need that kind of company today.

In twenty minutes they were at the park. Everett had been wise to advise her to wear Alaskas; the snow was quite deep, and the path where cleared was lumpy gray ice. The wide stone steps were especially treacherous, and Everett kept his hand securely beneath Marian's elbow as they slowly descended into the wooded valley. At least the bluff blocked the winds when they proceeded down the stairs.

His continuing silence let her thoughts roam free to examine the revelation that had burst upon her earlier this afternoon. She'd known for months that she was growing more and more attracted to Everett. Her respect and admiration for him knew few bounds, and in spite of the often remote attitude he assumed in her presence, she valued what friendship they shared. She longed for him to let down his silly defenses against women and allow their friendship to deepen.

Only now she knew it wasn't friendship she felt for Everett. She was in love with him. She wanted to share his struggles, his joys, and his pain.

Never had she considered such a sharing in her other relationships with men. Shame washed over her as she recognized that until now, she'd been concerned only with what the men and boys in her life could give her, not what she could offer them.

Even with Justin she'd cared only that he catered to her every whim, that he was one of the wealthiest men in River's Edge and spent money on her freely. Why, he'd even allowed her to choose the design for the home he'd built with the expectation they'd live in it together, and then gave her freedom to decorate it as she wished. She'd spent money on the house with an abandon that seemed frivolous now that she was seeing poverty first hand among the people who came to the mission.

Marian was glad to see when they neared the valley floor that they had the snow-filled glen to themselves. Not too surprising, considering the season.

At the bottom of the steps, Everett's hold on her arm dropped, and he caught her gloved hand in his own when they turned to their left toward the creek below the falls. She loved the way his hand in its thick glove swallowed her own, making her feel secure and as though they were joined more than by physical touch alone.

It was a minute before they could see the falls, as the bluff slanting between the steps and the creek hid from view the falls that were the heart of the valley. But when they reached the wooden bridge, its walk and rails piled with undisturbed snow, the glory of the falls in winter burst upon them.

She gasped in delight when sunlight dazzled off the frozen falls, and followed Everett slowly to the middle of the narrow footbridge, where the view was uninterrupted, never taking her gaze from the wonder before them.

"I've never seen anything so beautiful." She hadn't intended for it to come out in a whisper. She felt his gaze upon her, but was too entranced by the sight before them to return it.

His hold on her hand tightened, adding to her joy. *This will always be one of the most beautiful memories of my life.* She wanted to drink in every minuscule part of the loveliness: the falls frozen solid in their winter wonder, the quick little chirps of the birds as they hunted the nearby bushes in hopes of formerly missed seeds and berries, the cracking sound that filled what is so often called the silence of winter, and the feel of

Everett's touch enveloping her hand.

Minnehaha Falls was encased in ice from the top of the Trenton limestone ledge over which it tumbled to the pool where the creek bed continued on its winding journey through the wild glen. It was a fascinating combination of slender, foot-wide icicles, huge, wave-like masses of snow-covered ice, and pinnacles of ice wider than a man's body standing proudly from the lower creek bed to the top of the bluff.

Everett dropped her hand, and for the first time she felt the day's chill.

He studied her face for a moment, solemnly, and then turned toward the falls, leaning against the railing. Marian watched the soft balls of snow drift from the railing where his hands unconsciously knocked it from its perch to form punchy little holes in the snowy ice-covered creek bed below.

"For years I've come here when I needed to be alone."

It was the first time he'd spoken since they'd left the house. *But you're not alone this time,* she thought.

His gaze stayed locked on the sparkling, ice-covered falls.

"When you told me about Aurelia this afternoon. . ." he started, and then stopped.

She waited for him to continue.

He swallowed, and the sound was loud in the snow-quiet. "I had no idea she could see all the anger and bitterness inside me." He turned his head just enough to glance at her from hooded eyes. One corner of his firm, uncompromising mouth lifted in the imitation of a smile. "You'd think with the many times you've reminded Mrs. Dorothy and me over the last few months that children watch adults closely, that I would have realized before this that Aurelia might see more than the way I walk and talk."

His gaze slid back to the scenic beauty before them. "But she didn't read me quite right. My heart hasn't cried in years. It's been frozen as solid as those falls."

His comparison drew her gaze to the wall of ice, and instead of the beauty she'd seen before, she only felt their unrelenting chill. A shiver ran through her, and she drew her arms in tightly to her sides, though she knew that wouldn't warm her.

Everett's hands clutched the railing now. A ragged breath tore through him and ripped a hole in her heart.

Setting his broad shoulders firmly, he looked directly into her eyes, and she couldn't have looked away if her life had depended upon it. "I'd like to tell you how it was for Aurelia and me. If you don't want to hear it, say so, and I'll stop. It's not a pretty story."

"I'm here, Everett."

At her low comment, something leaped in his eyes.

And then they were shuttered again.

"I married Aurelia's mother soon after graduating from the University. In spite of my degree, I'd found I enjoyed working with my hands, and with the mission. That's what I was doing when we married. My wife was young, only seventeen, and perhaps I should have been wise enough to know that she didn't believe me when I said I planned to spend my life in the work I'd started."

He paused, and minutes passed before he continued.

"She hadn't expected the life I gave her. She wanted a husband whose career and income would give her a reflected respect, and a more elevated social station. She wanted fun times and a lot of laughs and the pretty things money can buy for a woman.

"After a couple years, she began to believe I wasn't going to leave the mission. By then, we were expecting Aurelia."

His lips compressed so tightly they could have been used for a vise. "She discovered she didn't want children, either. She didn't like being tied down by a baby, didn't like having someone dependent upon her, didn't like waiting on a child hand and foot.

"So when a more interesting prospect came around, she left."

Surely he didn't mean. . .not that she actually abandoned him and Aurelia? "You mean, she requested a divorce?" She didn't know anyone who had actually been divorced.

"No. She never got around to getting a divorce. She just left." Bitterness and sarcasm fought each other for supremacy in his voice, and the shock of his statement left her speechless.

"She moved into a nice, expensive apartment which was paid for by one of the wealthy young men who frequents the society parties you and Paget attend. After a time he tired of her. He stopped paying her rent and buying her expensive clothes and taking her to expensive restaurants. So she found another man to pay for them. And so it went, until she contracted a disease from one of her *friends,* and none of the young men wanted her around any more."

Horrified by his story, Marian could barely get her breath. One hand slid to her throat. She'd read in newspaper articles of women who acted in such an improper manner; she'd never suspected anyone she knew of having been married to such a woman! How could any woman have hurt Everett in such a manner? She struggled to keep back the words that rushed to her tongue.

He leaned heavily on the railing, and the muscles in his face looked like bands of iron beneath the skin. "So she came back."

In an almost emotionless voice, he told how he'd cared for her, how she'd asked after two weeks to have Aurelia taken away so the child wouldn't disturb her—and had made certain Aurelia knew she wasn't wanted, how Aunt Dorothy had taken Aurelia in during his wife's last months, and how he had cared for his wife, staying away from his work for weeks at a time.

Before he was through, Marian's hands circled one of his arms, and she leaned slightly against his side in an unconscious sign of her desire to comfort him. How he must have loved his wife to care for her after all the pain she'd given him!

"Kids can be incredibly cruel, even at a very young age.

Neighborhood kids and kids at the mission began repeating some of the things they heard their parents saying about my wife. Aurelia didn't understand anything, of course, except that her mother didn't love her or want her."

He hasn't called her by name once, only "my wife" or "Aurelia's mother."

"The bitterness that came with my wife's betrayal became as much a part of me as my arms or my legs."

"You must have loved her a great deal."

His gaze shifted uneasily. "I could hardly leave my own wife and the mother of my child out on the streets, regardless of what she'd done."

"Many men would have done just that, I expect."

He didn't reply. He stared at the falls with eyes that looked so angry Marian wondered that his gaze didn't melt them and restore the veil of falling water they'd seen last October.

She wasn't sure how much time had passed before he responded, but her fingertips had grown cold in their fur-lined kid gloves.

"For a long time, I thought I'd forgiven my wife. Then I saw the joy in your life, a joy that wasn't destroyed by the broken trust with your fiance. I began to realize I hadn't forgiven her.

"I thought God owed me for living up to my obligations as a husband in spite of the way my wife hurt me.

"It wasn't until you told me about your experience with Justin that I understood. You said we needed to live life the way it is, not the way we wished it would be, remember?"

She nodded.

"I wanted life to be what I saw as fair. I had no right to be angry at God because my wife didn't love us. As a Christian, loving her, caring for her, and forgiving her were all things I was to do regardless of her response. God doesn't promise people will love us back."

"No, but He promises to be with us, strengthen us, and comfort us."

His thickly gloved fingers absently massaged her own where her hand lay on his arm. His brow wrinkled into furrows, and she knew he was struggling to express his thoughts.

"I've known most of my life that we can never be good enough to demand God give us eternal life. That is a gift He presents us for believing in His Son, and accepting His love." He shook his head slowly. "How could I have thought my good deeds could buy anything else from God, even my wife's love and loyalty?"

"We all fall into that manner of thinking at times."

He began walking slowly back toward the steps, his hand still covering hers. "I've been trying to eliminate the bitterness with God's help, and I know I'm making progress, but it's slow. It's become such a part of my thinking. I have to keep reminding myself to forgive.

"But what's important now is Aurelia. I don't want her life to be warped by my bitterness and lack of trust."

"Aurelia already has a very sensitive spirit. As you allow God to continue working the bitterness out of your life, I believe Aurelia will see the change in you, and you'll see your change reflected in her."

She hesitated, wondering whether she dared ask the question in her mind. "Have you ever discussed your wife with Aurelia?"

"Not since she died. I thought it would be too painful for her."

"Keeping her fears to herself can be painful, too."

After a long moment he said, "I'll talk with her."

She wondered whether he could forgive a woman whose name he refused to use. Hesitantly she said, "You haven't told me your wife's name."

The fingers on hers tightened. "Charity. Her name was Charity."

Charity. Love. Somehow, it made her betrayal of Everett and Aurelia seem worse.

She knew life wasn't fair, but she wished it had been in this case. She hated the pain Everett and Aurelia had endured.

"You've been very good for Aurelia, you know."

She smiled. "Aurelia has been very good for me. I adore her."

"I. . .thank you for all you've done for her."

"You don't need to thank me, Everett. I love her, too."

On the first stair, she turned to him, surprising him into an abrupt halt. Thanks to the step, their faces were almost equal height. She smiled at him gently, wanting desperately to reach out and lay a hand along his firm, tense cheek.

"The falls won't stay frozen forever, Everett. The ice will thin, and begin to melt, and then chunks will fall and be washed away by the creek, and soon—very soon, only a month or two from now—the Laughing Water will be back."

Everett was decidedly more relaxed on the way back than she'd seen him in a long time, and he even "let down" to the extent of telling her a funny story.

She was still laughing at it when they entered the house, and Philander Paget's voice, in conversation with Dorothy, came loudly from the parlor.

Marian whirled about, looking up at Everett with shocked eyes above her gloved fingertips. "Oh, he'll be furious! I forgot he was coming!"

A comment which gave Everett a great deal of satisfaction for the rest of the evening.

thirteen

Marian's prediction of spring returning the Laughing Waters had been accurate, of course. Spring came sooner than expected to Minnesota. By the end of the first week in March, pussy willows were bursting forth. Record highs were recorded. The frozen ground began to thaw.

By mid-March, when the temperatures were reaching unheard of highs in the mid-seventies, Aurelia was already urging Everett to spend their Sunday afternoons at Minnehaha Falls.

The ice had disappeared from the creek and its wooded banks, and Everett knew it was disappearing from his mind and heart also. He was more relaxed than he'd been in years. Resting in God's forgiveness and grace himself made it easier for him to leave his wife in God's hands, too, and move on. To his surprise, he began to pity his wife, and wish he'd done more to bring joy to her short life. Mostly he wished that she'd experienced the peace of knowing God's forgiveness herself.

For a long time he'd thought he'd already forgiven his wife, that it was only natural to remain distrustful of women in particular and bitterly expectant that life would be unfair and hard. Besides, staying bitter helped him protect himself against other painful emotions—like risking broken trust once more.

Working through the memories, he was surprised at all the nice ones he'd forgotten, the times he and Charity had been happy together, before the years of disillusionment. Recalling them was healing.

Worst of all was the thought that perhaps if he hadn't been so certain he was right and righteous in the life he'd chosen for himself, he might have given his wife's needs more attention and prevented the pain her leaving had brought to all their lives. For it wasn't only himself and Aurelia who'd been hurt by her abandonment, but the life she chose away from them had brought physical and emotional pain on her also.

Aurelia was smiling more often these days. Looking back, he could see she'd begun to change soon after Marian's arrival. His recent change was having its own positive effect on her, however. One day after much prayer and worry, he'd followed Marian's advice and talked with Aurelia about the woman who had hurt them. He struggled to give his daughter good memories of her mother to go along with the painful ones. He'd never spoken harshly of his wife in front of Aurelia, but neither had he spoken kindly of her since she'd left them. He'd thought it easier on Aurelia not to discuss her at all, thought her too young to understand everything that was happening. Maybe it would have been better for Aurelia if he'd tried to talk about it occasionally, but he'd done the best he'd known to do at the time.

He often wondered what he and Aurelia would do when Marian left Mrs. Dorothy's home. He'd long given up hope of keeping his heart from being torn apart when she left, but not once did he allow his mind to linger on the tempting idea of courting her. He'd push it away and concentrate on enjoying her company from day to day, thankful for the time they could live almost as brother and sister beneath Mrs. Dorothy's roof.

One of the unusually warm March days, Everett crossed the playground between his shop and the kindergarten building, pleasantly surprised to find himself following a group of energized children Marian was attending. The spring weather brought out the children's exploring spirits, and Marian had told him how difficult it was becoming to keep them occupied inside with blocks, balls, card sewing, and story hours.

He followed the group at a little distance, nodding at two of the other assistants who passed on their way to the playground with excited groups of their own. He stopped beside the open door of the kindergarten room, watching Marian try to restore the wriggling, giggling bodies to order, and felt contentment fill him just to see her doing what she loved. His hands slid casually into his jeans' pockets, and he leaned lazily against the door frame, being careful to keep from distracting either Marian or the children with his presence.

Most of the children were finally settled about the table that still amazed him every time he saw its low height, when one of the boys stopped before Marian with eyes sparkling with smiling mischief. Dust covered his trousers and hands, and his straight hair was in boyish disarray, but Marian didn't scold, she merely smiled down at him.

Everett smiled too, because the child was all boy, and reminded him of every boy he'd known when he was that age.

"What can I do for you, Erik?"

The boy's grin stretched across his dirty face. "I have something for you, Miss Ames."

Everett swallowed the laugh that swelled up inside him at her skeptical look. She was learning to know boys, all right.

"What is it, Erik?"

"Close your eyes, and hold out your hands."

The other children were all attention now, and several of the other boys were giggling uncontrollably, some trying to hide their laughter behind their hands.

"Maybe I'd best keep my eyes open." But she gamely held out her hands, palms up.

"No, it's a surprise. You have to close them."

Everett watched her struggle with the idea of saying she'd rather not have the surprise, which was definitely a wise course of action, he thought. In the end, she gave in to Erik.

Everett jerked upright when Erik pulled a small garden snake from his pocket and dropped the twisting creature into Marian's hands. Marian's eyes and mouth flew open, and Everett took an impulsive step into the room.

"Oh!" Her gaze was glued to the harmless snake no wider than her thumb and less than a foot long, wrapping itself around her fingers.

Would Marian welcome his assistance or consider it interference? Everett forced himself to stay where he was. The snake wouldn't harm her, only frighten her a bit.

In a moment she'd hurried the few feet to the sand box in the corner of the room, and the dropped the green and yellow slithering object into a tin pail, covering the pail with a chipped china plate from a nearby table. Everett almost cheered her quick thinking.

The boys in the room were in stitches by now, shouting with laughter while the girls screamed.

Marian brushed the palms of her hands together ineffectually and wrinkled her nose in distaste before pasting a bright smile on her face and turning back to the children.

"Well, now! Erik certainly found us a sign of springtime, didn't he? Can any of you tell me where snakes live?"

All of the boys' hands shot into the hair, and some of the girls' lifted their arms timidly. In spite of the hands, the children didn't all wait to be called upon, but called out their answer eagerly. "In the ground!"

"That's right. Do people live in the ground, too?"

Giggles filled the room. "No!"

"Where do people live?"

"In houses!"

Smiling, Everett continued on his way to the cafeteria. She'd handled the situation beautifully. Most women would have dropped the snake, screamed at the top of their lungs, and worked the little girls into a frenzy while they were at it. Instead she'd turned it into a learning situation, and certainly not least, had won the respect of every boy in the room. He strongly suspected every one of them would have a "crush" on her for a good long while, and the tale of her bravery would pass down to other boys for years.

When classes were over he made his way back to the kindergarten room. Keeping his mind away from Marian had been more difficult than usual, and he was glad to see the room empty except for her.

She was wiping her hands off with a wet rag when he entered, scrubbing them so hard he suspected she might rub off a few layers of skin. He walked over to her, taking the rag and gently wiping her hands himself.

She didn't stop him, just looked up at him with her eyes more enormous than he'd ever seen them, large pools of blue that had deepened almost to navy. *Poor thing, the shock was beginning to set in now that the children were gone.*

"Has Aurelia left with Dorothy?"

She nodded.

"Where are Jessie and the other assistants?"

"In the cafeteria."

If she didn't stop trembling, he wouldn't be able to keep from pulling her into his arms to comfort her.

"Do you have a dry towel?"

She pulled her hands from his and opened a cupboard. To his disappointment, she dried her hands herself, her back to him. The large navy bow quivering at the nape of her neck was evidence she was still trembling, and hesitantly, he rested his hands on her shoulders.

"I saw the snake episode. You handled it perfectly."

She dropped the towel and turned around, and her nearness made the blood buzz in his ears. Her dainty hands were clutched at her breast. "My heart is still racing."

So was his, but for another reason!

Almost before he realized what he was doing, he'd pulled her gently into his arms, one hand cradling the back of her head, her hair's silkiness wonderful against his cheek. "It's behind you now."

She pushed against him gently, and with regret spilling through him, he allowed her to step back, though he kept his hands lightly on her elbows to steady her. "I'll be fine in a moment, truly I will."

"Of course you will." He slipped a knuckle beneath her chin and urged her face upward until he could smile brightly into her eyes. "You've won the hearts of those boys, you know. You'll be the topic at every one of their dinner tables tonight, you and your bravery."

The wobbly smile she returned him caught at his heart, and he couldn't keep from thinking how he'd like to kiss her. "A man could easily love you, Marian Ames."

He hadn't intended to say the words aloud! Mortified, he stared at her, wishing he could take the words back. Would she think him brutishly forward?

She surprised him by widening her shaky smile, and glancing shyly into his eyes. "I should hope so, Mr. Starr. At least, one man."

He hoped she meant him, and wasn't speaking hypothetically, for he couldn't resist touching his lips to that tender, trembling mouth. Wonder flowed through him when she leaned lightly against his chest, and returned his kiss.

It was over all too soon, and he searched her eyes, delighted and amazed and confused to see that she wasn't a bit embarrassed or insulted, but indeed, looked calmer than he about what had just happened between them!

"Marian?"

At his gruff whisper, she moved out of his arms, though she softened the move with her smile. "I. . .I wonder whether you'd remove the snake to the outdoors for me."

Her breathless reminder of the world about them made him want to kick himself. He'd never even asked to court her, and he'd brazenly held her and kissed her in a public room where any of the people with whom they worked could have entered and found them in an intimate embrace!

"I'm sorry." He walked abruptly across the room and picked up the tin pail, fury at himself keeping him company and making him feel more of a fool with every step. He was almost at the door when a skinny man of about thirty wearing a brown bowler and a brown and beige checked sack suit entered.

The man's little brown eyes behind round wire spectacles swept the room from the doorway with a busy, almost nervous gaze. "Could either of you direct me to Miss Marian Ames?"

Marian crossed the room toward him. "I'm Miss Ames."

Everett noticed the pencil and notebook in the man's hands, and alarm crept across his chest.

The man touched the fingers clutching his pencil to the front of his bowler. "I'm Benton from the *Minneapolis Tribune*. I wonder if you'd answer a few questions for me."

Everett set the pail on the low table beside him with a clang, not taking his gaze from the reporter.

"If you wish to ask about the kindergarten, Miss Jessie Watkins would be able to answer your questions more intelligently. I'm only an assistant."

"It's not the kindergarten I wish to speak of," Benton said impatiently. "I'm here about Rasmus Pierce."

Rasmus Pierce! Everett's gaze sought Marian's face. Why would the reporter want to ask her about that infamous criminal?

"I. . .I have nothing to say concerning Mr. Pierce."

Her sudden pallor frightened Everett, particularly in light of the snake episode that had already taken its toll on her nerves.

Impatience filled the skinny reporter's face, his bunching eyebrows knocking his glasses part-way down his nose. "But Miss Ames—"

Everett was in front of Benton in two steps, his wide chest

blocking the reporter's view of Marian. "The lady has told you she has nothing to say. I suggest you leave."

"Look here, mister! I'm just doing my job. Now if you'll step out of the way—"

Everett stepped out of the way. He grabbed the smaller man's arm firmly and hurried him from the room and down the hall toward the front door, the man babbling all the way about doing his job and filing assault charges.

Back in the kindergarten room, he went to Marian immediately. His hands on her shoulders, he searched her face to prove to himself she was all right in spite of her assurance that she was fine.

Her eyes held a sorrow and fear that cut into his chest.

"Everett, I. . ."

His hands framed her face. "You don't have to tell me anything. Nothing. Understand?"

She nodded at his fierce whisper. He dropped her face, picked up the tin pail, and left the room.

Yet in spite of his declaration, distrust and fright wriggled into his mind and chest. He recalled that Rasmus Pierce had been captured last fall in River's Edge, Marian's home town. It was obvious from her reaction to Benton's statement that there was some connection between her and Pierce. Had she been a victim of his crimes?

That had to be it, he assured himself, watching the snake disappear into the winter-dead grass at the edge of the playground.

The thought didn't settle the dread taking root in his stomach.

fourteen

Marian was glad Everett had a woodworking class that evening, and therefore wasn't able to escort her home. The long April daylight made it safe for her to make her way herself, and she needed the time to sort out her emotions.

She barely noticed the workmen and women making their way home from their jobs, most of the men chewing the popular *snus* and carrying their tin lunch pails. Budding leaves and early blossoming daffodils delicately scented the breeze, blending with the familiar pine smells of the sawmills, sweaty-horse smell from laboring sawmill and tradesmen's beasts, and the ever-present river odor.

Her conscious mind was oblivious to all of it, aware only of Everett and of the newsman's bold question. Where had the reporter heard that she knew Rasmus? What else did he know? Most important, what would Everett think if he discovered she'd been engaged to the criminal?

Dear Everett. When he'd pulled her into his arms and kissed her, only a short hour ago, she'd felt as though the entire world had come right. Nothing in her experience had been as sweet.

Then he'd said, "I'm sorry," and turned quickly away. Her heart had dropped to the floor in dismay. Did he think his actions a mistake? Didn't he realize she welcomed his advances? Perhaps he'd reacted on impulse in kissing her, and then apologized because the kiss meant nothing to him.

No, she couldn't believe that of Everett. He wasn't the type of man who played with women's affections. He would never allow himself to display emotion which he didn't feel for a woman.

Which fact made everything worse. If he cared for her, learning of her and Rasmus would hurt him, and that was the last thing in the world she wanted.

Dorothy met her in the hallway just inside the door, a yellow envelope in her hand, and an anxious look on her usually calm face. "This came for you a few minutes ago."

Marian stared at it for a long moment before slowly reaching to take it from Dorothy. *A telegram. It couldn't be good news.*

Taking a deep breath, she opened it, scanning the contents quickly. She bit her lips to keep back the moan that rose in her throat, and handed the yellow slip of paper to her aunt. "It's from Father. Rasmus Pierce's trial begins in River's Edge Monday, and I'm to be called as a witness."

"Monday! My dear, you'll need to leave immediately!"

"Tomorrow morning, yes." Suddenly cold, Marian crossed her arms over her chest. "If you don't mind, I. . .I should like to tell Everett myself the reason for my departure."

"Of course, dear." Dorothy hugged her gently, and the lavender scent Marian always associated with her aunt surrounded her comfortingly. "*Vår Herre är bra att ha när åskan går.*"

Marian smiled slightly. "One of Sonja's proverbs."

"Yes." Dorothy's small hands still rested on Marian's shoulders.

"What does it mean?"

"'It is good to have our Lord when it thunders.'"

"Yes, yes, it is."

And what would the Lord have her tell Everett, she wondered, for it would surely thunder then.

She withdrew early to her room to pack, and to be alone to consider the situation and pray. No matter that the idea frightened her, she must tell Everett. She could at least show him that much respect. It would be worse if he heard of it from someone else.

Having made her decision gave her peace. She would tell

him this evening, when he came home from the mission and after Aurelia was in bed.

Only he didn't come home at the usual time. Aurelia, Sonja, and Dorothy were all in bed when the tall clock in the hallway chimed eleven, and Marian slowly climbed the steps to her room. She couldn't imagine what could be keeping him so long. He'd never returned so late. She was tempted to continue waiting up for him, but he would be exhausted when he arrived. It was no time to burden him with her dreadful news.

From her bed, she heard the single *bong* of the hall clock sounding the hour of one only moments before she heard the front door open. Everett must have arrived home. "Thank you, Lord," she whispered into the dark, not realizing until that moment she'd been afraid for Everett's safety.

Knowing he was home didn't calm all her fears. The peace which had come from her decision earlier had slipped away while she waited to speak to Everett, and she spent a restless night.

⠦

Her trial with Everett began earlier than she expected. He was dreadfully quiet at the breakfast table, even for him, and he never had been a talkative man. He gave Aurelia any attention she wished, politely responded to Dorothy's conversational attempts, and thanked Sonja for the meal.

He didn't look at Marian once.

Marian could barely swallow her toast and marmalade. Her throat was too thick with threatening tears at his so obviously ignoring her presence.

When the uncomfortable meal was completed, Dorothy smiled at Aurelia and rose. "Won't you come up to my room with me and look at some special linens I'm thinking of using for the luncheon next week?" Taking the child's hand, she continued blandly, "Your papa and Marian have some things to discuss, and we'd only be bored by their conversation."

Everett's head jerked toward her at the comment, but Dorothy was giving her full attention to Aurelia, and in a moment the two had left the room.

Everett's gaze shot to Marian, his usually rich brown eyes black as the sky before a thunderstorm. Every plane of his face was tense.

Marian almost abandoned her plan in the face of his naked hostility, but she knew if she did so she'd live to regret it.

She'd thought he was avoiding eye contact with her because he was sorry he'd kissed her and spoken of love yesterday, but surely that couldn't be the cause of such fury. What had she done? Had Dorothy told him of Rasmus and the trial after all?

No, Aunt Dorothy wouldn't do that. She respected another's privacy more than anyone else Marian knew.

Her fingers in her lap played with the edge of the white linen tablecloth, and she took a deep breath. "I. . .I would like to speak with you, if you will allow me a few minutes of your time."

He crossed his arms over his chest and leaned back in the stiff dining room chair, his gaze never leaving hers. "I'm listening."

Before she could begin, Sonja entered through the swinging door to clear the table. The maid picked up a plate with a slice of cold toast remaining on it, straightened and looked from Marian to Everett and back again uncertainly.

Marian stood slowly. "Perhaps we could speak in the parlor, so Sonja may continue with her duties." She smiled tremulously at him, hoping Sonja wouldn't realize how strained things were between them.

He rose silently and indicated with one hand that he would follow her.

The parlor was cool with no fire in the fireplace, but Marian doubted a fire would warm her. She seated herself stiffly at one end of the divan, her hands clenched in her lap.

Her heart sank even further when Everett sat down in his favorite overstuffed chair, over six feet away. This was going to be difficult enough without yelling across the room.

He rested one ankle on his opposite knee and crossed his arms again, as though he wished to visually reinforce the wall he'd built between them. His gaze was once more locked with hers and his mouth was so taut that she thought irrelevantly that if it were a violin string, it would break.

Swallowing her pride, she began. "This is very difficult for me. There is something I feel you have the right to know, and I ...I would rather you heard it from me than from someone else."

He didn't move a muscle, only continued glaring at her.

She licked her lips, which were suddenly dry as tinder. "I received a telegram yesterday evening from my father. Rasmus Pierce's trial is to begin next week, and I'm to testify."

His eyes didn't show the slightest flicker of surprise, and uneasiness slithered through her stomach. *He couldn't know yet,* she tried unsuccessfully to reassure herself.

"I told you I was engaged to Justin. When he arrived home from Chicago two days before our wedding already married to Constance, I was hurt and furious. Childishly, the only thing I could think of was hurting him as badly as he'd hurt me. Rasmus Pierce's family is from River's Edge, and I knew Rasmus cared for me, so I. . .I. . ."

She couldn't say it. It was the last thing on earth she wanted Everett to know. Tears pooled in her eyes until his form was wavy before her. She opened her eyes wider to keep the tears from overflowing. She didn't want him to think she was using tears for his sympathy.

She struggled for control of her voice, which threatened to be as rich with tears as her eyes. "To heap revenge on Justin, I became. . .engaged. . .to Rasmus." The last words were a mere whisper.

"I know."

Everett's two words were so hard she thought he could as easily have thrown rocks at her as speak. She blinked furiously, only a couple tears dribbling over her bottom lashes, surprise effectively drying the rest.

"How did you know?"

"The reporter came back to the mission last night. He told me he wanted to speak to Pierce's fiancée—to you. I didn't believe him at first, called him all kinds of a liar and thought a few other things about him I'm not too proud to remember now, but by the time he was through presenting his case, I knew it was true."

"Becoming engaged to Rasmus was a foolish thing to do." Her fingers twisted the navy blue serge skirt. "I broke the engagement after only a few days."

Everett pushed himself from his chair. "I don't wish to hear the grimy details."

She flinched at the harshness of his voice.

He began pacing the room, his heels sounding loud even through the thick Brussels carpet. One hand rubbed the back of his neck. "I must be the world's top fool. The only two women in the world I've cared for prefer men who live on society's dirty fringes." He snorted. "And what does that say about my ability to judge the fairer sex?"

"I never cared for Rasmus, not for a moment. I'm ashamed to say I only used his affection for me to my own purposes."

He loomed in front of her, breathing hard, clenching his fists at his side. If it had been anyone but Everett, she would had been terrified. "I'm not laying my heart on the line again. I let one woman plow it to bits; I'm not about to let you do the same. Go to the trial. When you return, Aurelia and I will be gone."

She shot to her feet, grasping his arm. "You can't leave because of me! This is your home."

He looked pointedly at her hand until, flushing hotly, she removed it from his arm. His gaze moved back to hers. "This *was* my home."

She watched him leave, wondering whether it was possible for one's chest to burst from sheer sorrow. Then she dropped to the divan, burying her face in her hands.

Minutes later she felt the divan cushion dip slightly when Dorothy sat down beside her. One small hand began gently rubbing her shoulder.

"He hates me, Aunt Dorothy!" she whispered through her sobs.

"Shhh, dear. He doesn't hate you."

"You didn't hear him." She relayed the conversation in a voice that jerked and trembled around her tears.

"It was his pain speaking, child. He's trying to protect himself from hurting. He needs time to unravel everything."

"He will never forgive me."

"Of course he shall. Do you recall the Swedish proverb Sonja used to explain Aurelia's mistrust of young women who reminded her of her mother? 'A burnt child shuns the fire.' Adults shun the fire, also. Eventually he will realize that you are not like his wife, and will know that your love won't cause him the pain he fears."

Marian brushed the moistness from her cheeks with the palms of her hands and sniffed rather inelegantly. "Is my love for him so obvious?"

A soft smile touched Dorothy's gentle face. "No more obvious than his love for you."

Marian shook her head. "I'd thought he might be learning to love me, but I'm afraid I've destroyed any hope of that."

Dorothy's hand smoothed the hair at the side of Marian's head. "To youth, it may look that way. But with the experience of my years, I believe you are mistaken. Everett needs time, dear. There is nothing you can do to change that. God seldom changes people's feelings overnight. He gives us time to think things through, and weigh them, and learn what is important and what is real and lasting, and what is not. It is a process we cannot rush, and is often painful. Everett is a good, wise man. He will allow himself to love you, eventually."

"Does growing always hurt this much?"

"Growth often comes through our pain, yes."

"Well, I hope God will not consider this irreverent, but I dearly hope I am through growing for awhile."

Dorothy's soft laugh had a thankfully calming effect on Marian's nerves.

The door to the hall opened, and Sonja slipped just inside the room to announce Philander's arrival.

Marian brushed a leftover tear from her face impatiently. "Whatever is he doing here?"

"I don't know, Miss Marian."

"I didn't mean to snap at you, Sonja, I was simply speaking my thoughts aloud." She turned pleading eyes to Dorothy. "I don't believe I'm up to seeing him at the moment."

She wasn't given a chance to decline. The parlor door was flung back before Dorothy could reply, and Philander strode into the room.

With a soft sigh of resignation, Marian rose. "Thank you, Sonja." She squeezed Dorothy's hand. "And thank you."

When the women had left the room, Marian invited Philander to be seated. He refused, and she remained standing also.

Gray bowler and leather gloves in one hand, he faced her. "I received the message you sent to the house last evening, saying you are leaving the city for a few days, and shall not be keeping our engagement this evening."

"Not *shall* not, but cannot."

One corner of his mouth twitched impatiently, and he knocked his hat softly against his thigh. "I thought you understood how important this evening is to me. Mr. Blatten, the law firm's head partner, is seriously considering me for a junior partnership. The party at his home this evening promises to be one of the social highlights of the season. You know how highly Blatten thinks of you. Your presence at my side is most important."

"I'm sorry, Philander, but I cannot attend." As succinctly as possible, she explained the situation. Strangely, it did not disturb her at all to tell him, and it had seemed very nearly the end of the world to tell Everett. Of course, Philander was also from River's Edge, and though they'd never discussed Rasmus, she felt sure he'd heard of her former engagement.

If he *had* heard of it, he had forgotten it, she realized shortly.

"You are going to testify at that rapscallion's trial? The entire civilized world will hear you were engaged to him!"

"I hardly think the news will spread that far."

"It will be in the Minneapolis newspapers."

She sighed deeply and linked her hands in front of her, thinking of Everett reading those same newspaper accounts. "Yes, I'm very much afraid it shall be."

"How can you be so calm about it?"

He fairly shouted with rage, and Marian turned her gaze on him in surprise.

"Philander, I have no choice but to testify."

"Do you not realize the detail with which the newspapers will cover this trial?"

"I should, after following some of the cases with which you've been involved over the last few months, but," she spread her hands helplessly, "I have no control over the newspaper reports."

"Rasmus is quite famous, as criminals go, and you're the niece of a prosperous Minneapolis businessman, *and* you have been tripping Minneapolis society on *my* arm all winter. Do you realize what the news of your engagement to Rasmus Pierce will do to my reputation?"

"Please, Philander, keep your voice down." It wasn't his loud voice that alarmed her as much as the fury in his face. He was quivering like an aspen in the wind, and even his cheeks shook. His face had grown so purple it looked stained with red wine.

He ignored her request, and she wondered whether he had even heard it. "When Blatten hears of your engagement to Pierce, all hope of a partnership for me in his firm will die an instant death, never to be resurrected. You shall destroy my career!"

He took a threatening step toward her, and she drew back, her eyes growing wide.

"That's far enough, Paget!"

Relief flooded her at Everett's even but firm voice. He filled the doorway. Never had anyone's presence been more welcome.

Philander flipped his hand toward the door. "I'll thank you to leave us alone, Starr. This is a private discussion."

Everett sauntered in. His tone was almost conversational compared to Philander's. "If you want your conversation to be private, I suggest you lower your voice. Every word you say can be heard on the top floor."

Philander pumped his small lips together. "That is no concern of yours."

"Since my five-year-old daughter lives in this house, it certainly is my concern. Regardless of the child's presence, there's never an excuse for a gentleman to speak to a lady in such a manner."

Marian wouldn't have thought such strength could be found in such a quiet voice. Philander must have recognized the iron beneath the soft sheath, also, she thought, for he recoiled a step, regarding Everett through narrowed lids.

"You don't understand the situation, Starr."

"I understand it perfectly. You are relying on Miss Ames' charms to further your career rather than on your own abilities as a lawyer."

Philander's head jerked back an inch, and he tried to look down his nose at Everett. "You are too uneducated to understand the business world."

"Philander!"

Both men ignored Marian's indignant exclamation.

"Perhaps you're correct," Everett replied with a smoothness that made Marian wonder what was to come next, "but I'm not too uneducated to know that your presence is unwelcome here."

Philander's gaze jerked to Marian. "Tell this person to leave us that we might continue our discussion."

She folded her hands at her waist and met his gaze evenly. "I'm sure I can't imagine what else you could possibly have to say."

Philander's mouth bounced open and shut three times before he finally pressed his lips together, slapped his hat on his thin hair, and stormed from the room.

Marian saw Sonja flash through the hall in her black dress and crisp white apron to open the front door for Philander. A moment later the door slammed shut, its glass rattling. When Sonja passed the parlor doorway a moment later, she was dusting her palms against each other smartly, and muttering, "*'Tomma tunnor skramla mest!'*"

To Marian's amazement, Everett chuckled.

"What did she say?"

"'Empty barrels make the loudest noise.'"

He was still chuckling when he'd left the room, but he hadn't looked at her once since he entered to challenge Philander. He would defend her, but not befriend her.

Marian didn't feel a whit like chuckling.

Before leaving to catch the train, she said goodbye to Aurelia, explaining she was going home for a short while, once again leaving the photograph album with the girl, and promising to write. Aurelia was sad to see her leave, but there were no doubts this time about her eventual return, and Marian didn't have to ask for the hug Aurelia offered. Marian couldn't help remembering Everett's promise to be gone when she returned, and wondered whether she'd ever again see the little girl who had become a part of her heart.

This time Everett didn't drive her to the depot; she took a covered cab. Waiting for the train to leave, seated on amethyst velvet upholstery, she leaned her forehead against the cool window pane, her gaze scanning the platform, hoping against hope Everett would relent and come to say goodbye.

He didn't.

fifteen

Entering the Winona County courthouse Monday morning with her parents, Marian shivered. The massive building of rough, contrasting colors of stone, with huge arches about its doors and deep-set windows, a castle-like tower rising high above the four-stories, gave an impression of cold impersonality. "Justice to be meted out based on the facts of the case, with no attention to the individuals involved," it seemed to say.

The prosecutor, a tall, wiry man with graying, curly hair and silver, round-rimmed glasses met Marian and her parents in the wide, high-ceilinged hallway outside the courtroom. He explained briefly that Marian would not be called for some time. First, the jury must be chosen, and the opening statements given. Even then, other witnesses would be called first, Justin and his wife among them.

The prosecutor excused himself and hurried to greet another group arriving at the top of the wide steps leading to the court floor. Marian recognized Justin among them, dressed in his customary gray business suit and bowler, looking as sober and distinguished as always. His wife, Constance, was beside him, her arm through his as comfortably as though they'd been together for years instead of months.

After a couple minutes, Justin and Constance stopped to speak with the Ames family, and Marian wondered briefly why she wasn't uncomfortable with the couple, considering their past. Instead, she found their calm, quiet natures reassuring.

Of course, Justin had always been a reassuring man to be around. At twenty-six, he was considerably older than Marian, and his attitude toward her had always been more brotherly than romantic. Even when he and Marian had been engaged, the most exciting thing about the man was the money in his command—a revealing truth about her own nature which made Marian squirm inside now.

From the way gentle Constance looked at him, his dark-haired wife found him very exciting, Marian thought. When Justin's gaze met his wife's, the admiration in his eyes brought a rosy glow to Constance's cheeks. Everett would never look at her in that endearing manner now.

In spite of that thought, a smile played on Marian's mouth as the Ameses and the Knights entered the courtroom and found seats. To think she and Justin and Constance were here to testify against Rasmus Pierce, and if it weren't for Rasmus, Justin and Constance would never have married, and she herself would never have fallen irrevocably in love with Everett. It seemed they owed the criminal a debt of gratitude!

Of course, that didn't erase Rasmus' robberies, shootings, and kidnappings.

The courtroom was full of curious bystanders, but the only people who made Marian nervous were the reporters and their accompanying artists who would supply sketches of Rasmus and the witnesses for the greedy newspapers. It made her sick to her stomach to remember how avidly she'd read reports of other trials. Now she would be part of the public's daily entertainment for days or weeks to come.

She tried not to think of the way Everett's face would look when he read the accounts, and especially not to imagine how betrayed he'd feel.

Marian and her parents joined Justin and Constance for lunch. When Marian first mentioned her work at the kindergarten, Justin's expression showed mild surprise, and she thought with distaste that he was justified in wondering that the childish woman to whom he'd once been engaged was involved in such a work. Respect soon replaced surprise as she told of her experiences. The couple from River's Edge were flatteringly interested in the mission, and plied her with questions about the manner in which the mission was run, its reception from the immigrants in the neighborhood, its importance during the current economic times, and Marian's opinion of the kindergarten efforts on the children's development.

The day ended with no one called to the witness stand. The jury was selected, and the opening statements given. Tomorrow the witnesses would begin sharing their experiences with the world.

Marian told herself she could rest in the Lord's hands, that He was sufficient to even this situation. Yet she slept restlessly, and wondered how long she would have to walk with Him to trust Him completely.

Looking into her dressing-room mirror the next morning and noting the blue circles beneath her eyes, she sighed. Trusting God was a lesson she hadn't learned well yet. She hoped learning it wouldn't be as painful as some of the other lessons she'd learned since recommitting her life to Him last fall.

That recommitment had been the result of responding to Rasmus' actions, too, she realized, with a small smile.

An unexpected peace pushed some of the despair from her heart at the thought. If God could bring so much good from Rasmus' intended evil actions, surely she could trust Him with this trial. Perhaps Everett had been hurt by her revelation of her past engagement to Rasmus, but God could heal him eventually, if he'd allow Him to do so. Most likely Everett would never allow himself to love her now, but if she'd allow it, God could even heal her broken heart. Look at Justin and Constance, after all.

Marian waited in the courthouse hallway with her parents until the last minute, dreading confinement in that room with an audience eagerly feasting on others' trouble. Her mother on one of her father's arms and herself on the other, they finally headed for the wide double doors.

It was then, out of the corner of her eye, she caught sight of him. Just a glimpse of a man in an inexpensive gray striped suit removing a smart new bowler, but she would know him anywhere.

Dropping her father's arm, she turned toward the top of the stairs, where Everett stood staring at her. Even from the distance she could see the uncertainty in his eyes, as though even now he questioned the wisdom of his presence.

She was barely aware of her father asking her what was the matter. It didn't occur to her answer. She simply waited, giving Everett time to come to her if he chose.

She saw the quick, firm set of his mouth just before he started across the marble floor. His hands reached for hers when he came close, and her heart rejoiced when they closed over her own.

Introductions were made to her parents, and her father, after quickly sizing up the young man, nodded to her. "Your mother and I will save you seats," he said, and her parents left them alone.

Everett had released her hands to shake hands with her father, and Marian wished desperately he'd reclaim them, but he didn't. He simply stood close before her, looking as tired as she'd felt upon arising that morning, his gaze burning into hers.

"I. . .I didn't want you to have to face this alone," he started stumblingly. "That is, I felt sure your parents would be here, but. . .I couldn't help thinking that I wouldn't want my life with Charity displayed to the public in this manner, and I couldn't bear the thought of your life being laid bare this way, of the pain it would cause you. I. . .thought it might help to have someone here who understood what you'll be going through."

"Thank you." Remembering the betrayal and anger he'd felt

at her revelation, she wished she could think of something to do or say to let him know she realized what a great sacrifice he was making for her.

His fingers bent the stiff rim of his new derby unconsciously. "I don't know what my presence here means beyond that. I won't mislead you; I'm not ready to trust again."

She glanced at the floor, lowering her lashes to prevent him seeing her disappointment. Her earlier realization that God could eventually heal the pain she'd inflicted on Everett didn't prevent her fervent wish that she had never caused it. "I understand, and I'm grateful for the support you've offered. It was kind of you to come."

She could see his fingers twisting the edge of his derby, and thought he would soon destroy his new hat, the most fashionable she'd seen him wear.

"If you like, I'll stay."

His gruff offer brought her gaze back to his in surprise. Determination and pain mingled in his rich brown eyes. *Would it only increase his pain to stay?* she wondered.

"I ought to release you from fulfilling that offer, but I'd like very much to have you stay."

He nodded sharply, as though to say it was settled, and offered her his arm on which to enter the courtroom.

Marian couldn't help but notice Rasmus, seated beside his lawyer. Arms crossed defensively over his chest, he scanned the jury, the reporters, and the audience with an impassive expression, until his gaze met hers. She didn't dare smile, for fear he would think she was laughing at his predicament, and he did not smile either. His gaze shifted to Everett, and she watched him study the man beside her for a few minutes. What was he thinking? Could he tell Everett meant a great deal to her?

When the judge was announced, Rasmus gave her one last, piercing look before standing and facing forward. She gave a soft sigh of relief. His attention to her had already drawn the unwelcome notice of the reporter, Benton.

The morning dragged for Marian. Sheriff Tucker from River's Edge was the first witness. His testimony drew out the basic facts of the case: the train robbery near River's Edge, the following robbery of Justin's bank, and the subsequent kidnapping of Constance's niece and nephew and Marian.

Justin and Constance's marriage and the reason for the kidnappings were not yet revealed, and Marian grew restless waiting for their revelation. Time wouldn't change the facts, and Everett, the only person whose reaction she truly cared about, already knew them.

It was bittersweet having him beside her. He listened intently to the testimony, offering no support other than his presence. He didn't smile at her, or squeeze her hands, or speak to her unnecessarily. It thrilled her that he cared enough to be there, but the knowledge he wasn't willing to risk his heart with her after the trial dampened the joy of his presence.

One of the Pinkerton men who had been involved with Rasmus' apprehension, Alexander Bixby, was the next to testify, but his testimony served only to substantiate the sheriff's testimony.

Justin was next. Marian didn't know whether to be relieved or not when the prosecution didn't draw out the facts surrounding Justin's marriage and the reasons for the kidnapping.

The defense wasn't as thoughtful. It was soon revealed that Rasmus had forced Justin and Constance, strangers at the time, to marry at gunpoint, to avoid Justin's marriage to Marian. Gasps rippled through the audience at the news, and as one, they leaned forward slightly in their seats. *Like a starving dog sighting a juicy bone,* Marian thought, her mouth tasting metallic from bitterness.

Everett had drawn a deep breath at the shock, also. From the corner of her eye, she watched him cross his arms and drop his chin to his chest, the muscles in his cheek working.

When asked why he and Constance hadn't immediately had the marriage annulled, Justin's gaze met Marian's briefly, and moved on to his wife before meeting the attorney's gaze. "He threatened to harm Constance's niece and nephew if we told anyone we hadn't entered into the marriage voluntarily."

This tidbit practically had the crowd licking their lips, Marian thought in disgust.

One of Everett's hands settled over hers where her string-gloved fingers were clutched together in her lap. She darted a look of gratitude at him and smiled weakly. He didn't return the smile, only squeezed her hands and returned his attention to the front of the room, though his hand remained on hers.

Constance was the next witness. The audience was thrilled to discover she'd been a Pinkerton agent assigned to the Rasmus Pierce case. Marian watched the reporters writing as fast as they could make their pencils move, and the artists sketching as quickly. Poor Constance and Justin, for Constance's likeness was sure to grace the front page of the Minneapolis and St. Paul newspapers tomorrow.

The day ended without Marian being called to the stand or her engagement to Rasmus being revealed. The thought of spending another day in the emotion-charged courtroom was in itself exhausting.

Marian introduced Justin and Constance to Everett before leaving the courthouse, but her concern was centered on the couple rather than Everett. "I'm truly sorry the details of your wedding came out in such an improper manner."

Justin glanced at Constance before replying. "Please don't concern yourself over it. We knew it was possible it would come out with the trial."

"Besides," Constance added, smiling sweetly, "the people of River's Edge have seen us as a family long enough not to hold the facts surrounding our wedding against us. It was you who gave us that reprieve of time last fall when you told the local newspapers that God knew we were meant to be together. We can never thank you enough for your generosity and forgiveness."

Marian felt Everett's intent gaze upon her and flushed, embarrassed at such praise. "There was never anything to forgive. One need only see the two of you together to know you are wonderful for each other."

Everett didn't ask for further details after Constance and Justin left, and Marian didn't offer them. Much to Marian's disappointment, he turned down her mother's invitation to have dinner with them, though they were all staying at the new Schlitz Hotel. However, he assured Marian he'd be at the courthouse again the next day.

Her eyes searched for him immediately upon arrival in the morning, and relief flooded through her when their gazes met and he was again at her side.

Although Marian's kidnapping had been revealed by the sheriff's testimony, the fact of her engagement had not yet been testified to. She knew from the prosecutor that it would likely not be brought up until she was herself on the witness stand, as from anyone else it would be considered hearsay. She'd also been warned that the defense attorney would consider the engagement a key part of Rasmus' defense regarding the kidnapping, since it was hardly conceivable that a man would forcefully detain his own fiancée.

When Marian was finally called to the stand, dread rooted her feet to the floor for a minute, and she felt the blood drain from her face. Everett squeezed her hand, and she turned her head slightly to meet his gaze. His face looked as pale as hers, his eyes almost fierce, but he whispered, "You can do this, Marian. Remember *Vår Herre*."

Vår Herre, Our Lord. "It is good to have our Lord when it thunders," Aunt Dorothy had said when they'd received the telegram about the trial.

She gave Everett a small, shaky smile and nodded, forcing herself to rise. She felt the reluctance with which he loosed his hold on her hand.

Try as she would to keep her gaze straight ahead, she glanced at Rasmus just before passing the table where he sat with his lawyer. He was watching her thoughtfully, one elbow on the table, his hand covering his bearded chin.

The defense attorney was not long in coming to the most personal and embarrassing portions of Marian's association with Rasmus. She kept her gaze on him rather than allowing it to stray to Everett or Rasmus, keeping her back straight and her hands folded quietly in her lap with an effort.

The stocky, balding attorney with the florid, drooping face began by reminding the court of Justin's testimony that Rasmus had forced his marriage to Constance to prevent his marriage to Marian. "And was that indeed the reason for this forced marriage, Miss Ames?"

"Yes."

Her acknowledgement was lost in the prosecutor's forceful objection. "Surely counsel realizes Miss Ames could not know the reason for the ceremony, since she was not present at it."

"Sustained."

Rasmus' attorney pressed his wide lips together and drew a deep breath.

Marian decided she would not be so quick to answer future questions, but would hesitate long enough for the prosecutor to have opportunity to prevent her offering unnecessary information.

"Very well," the defense continued, "then we shall go on to an event at which the witness surely was present, a proposal for her hand in marriage."

Marian kept her attention on the attorney, hoping she appeared calm. Silently, she sent up a prayer. The realization that Everett, Justin, and Constance were likely all praying for her lent comfort.

The attorney's beady eyes focused on her. "After Justin Knight married his present wife, did you become betrothed to Rasmus Pierce?"

She hesitated, glancing hopefully at the prosecuting attorney. He sat back in his chair, bouncing a fist off his chin lightly, and gave no indication there would be an objection this time.

Everyone in the room seemed to be holding their breath, waiting for her answer. She opened her lips to reply.

"No!" Rasmus' voice cracked in the quiet room.

Shocked, she grasped the arms of the chair and turned with the rest of the courtroom to Rasmus.

The judge's gavel banged repeatedly to restore order while the crowd gasped and whispered to one another. When quiet was restored, the judge demanded Rasmus make no further outbursts.

Rasmus rose, his fingertips resting on the table before him. "Yer honor, my attorney is evidently misinformed. I ain't never bin engaged to Miss Ames, and I can't 'low her ta be accused of sech."

Marian stared at him while the noise of the crowd swirled through the room once more, but Rasmus refused to look at her, keeping his gaze directly on the judge. The judge began pounding his gavel once more. Marian darted a glance at Rasmus' attorney, who looked as though he might experience apoplexy at any moment, his baggy jowls quivering.

When the room was once more quiet, the judge asked Rasmus whether he would like to speak with his attorney before questioning resumed.

Rasmus shot a glance at his attorney before looking back at the judge. He straightened his shoulders. "No, yer honor. I ain't never bin engaged ta Miss Ames." He waved a hand at the area filled by representatives of the press. "Can't hev my reputation ruined by lettin' the world think I'd be satisfied with one woman."

The smirk he gave added conviction to his comment.

This time the judge's gavel was accompanied by the threat to throw everyone out of the room except those immediately involved in the case. He pointed the useful end of the wooden tool at the defense attorney and demanded, "And you'll keep your client under better control in the future. I'm declaring a fifteen-minute break so you can confer with your client, something it appears you haven't done enough of before this trial began."

The rest of Marian's testimony was a disappointment to the crowd after Rasmus' sensational declaration. She merely revealed details of the kidnapping and rescue, omitting reference to her engagement to Rasmus, since neither the defense or prosecution questioned her concerning the same again.

The wonder of Rasmus' unexpected announcement stayed with her for the rest of the day. Why had he said that?

At five o'clock when everyone else was filing from the courtroom, Marian asked Everett if he would wait for her, and then asked the judge if she could speak with Rasmus. Reluctantly, he agreed, if she would speak in front of the defense attorney and prosecutor. She hesitated, then agreed to his stipulation.

Rasmus stood beside the defense table, his head back somewhat defiantly, his arms crossed over his chest, and his legs two feet apart. His face looked closed to her as solidly as though a door stood between them.

The defense attorney stood on one side of him, the prosecuting attorney stood beside her. Marian wished the conversation could be private, and wondered if Rasmus' defensive attitude was a result of their presence.

She smiled at him, trying to break the ice.

He didn't smile back.

Marian licked her lips nervously. "Why did you do it,

Rasmus?"

She didn't need to identify the action to which she referred.

A little of the stiffening in his jaw relaxed. "The things ya talked 'bout when ya came ta visit me at the lock-up, I bin thinkin' on 'em. Been readin' the Bible some, too. Not thet I've got religion or anythin', ya understand," he hurried to assure her, "but I got ta thinkin', seems I've done enough ta ya in the name of love. No reason ta do more. Jest 'cause I got a bee in my bonnet fer ya, no reason fer the whole countryside ta think a fine lady like you'd agree ta marry up with someone like me."

She smiled. "You haven't any 'religion' yet, though?"

The beginning of a smile fought at the edge of his mouth. His thin lips quivered to control it. "Naw." He shifted his weight on his feet. "Well, thinkin' on it, mebbe."

It was quite an admission from him, she realized, and tried to keep her smile small. If she made too much of it, his pride might keep him from continuing to "think on it."

With a lift of his head, he indicated Everett, who was leaning against the wall beside the door at the back of the courtroom. "He someone special?"

She followed his gaze and nodded. "Yes. At least, he's special to me. I'm not so sure my affections are returned."

Rasmus' gaze softened fractionally. "Hope he's worthy of ya."

"He's more than worthy of me. My concern, and possibly his, is that I may not be worthy of him."

Minutes later, Marian joined Everett and together they left the building. Justin and Constance were waiting outside in the pleasant spring evening. Marian breathed deeply of the air, alive with the smells of grass and trees and the nearby Mississippi—the same river which flowed near the mission.

No one asked what Marian had discussed with Rasmus. She expected they knew.

"It was untypically gentlemanly of Rasmus, what he did in court today," Justin offered.

"Yes." She smiled at him and his bride broadly. "However, he did tell me just now that when he forced you two to marry, it wasn't his intention to make Justin so happy."

Out of the corner of her eye she saw the frowning look Everett shot at her. She'd have to explain to him about Justin and Constance. Perhaps it would strengthen his trust in the Lord's goodness. If the Lord could bring such joy to Justin and Constance, who had been strangers when they married, surely He would eventually heal Everett and Aurelia if they'd allow it.

sixteen

The end of the first day.

Everett hung the small saw he'd finished cleaning on its wall peg, one hand lingering on the smooth wooden handle, and stared at it unseeingly. The first day back in Minneapolis after returning from the trial. It had been one of the longest days in his life.

How was Marian doing? Had he left too soon? What if the prosecutor was mistaken and her engagement would yet become public? He should have stayed longer, just in case.

His gaze shifted to Jules, diligently sweeping up sawdust and metal bits, reviving the pleasant pine odor of the wood that had been worked earlier.

Everett rubbed a hand along the back of his continually tense neck. He couldn't have stayed longer, barring a true need on Marian's part. He had responsibilities here: his work at the mission, the Newsboys' Club, and most importantly, Aurelia. Marian understood that.

Besides, the longer he stayed at Marian's side during the trial, the closer he came to risking everything.

He'd battled royally with himself over whether to go to the trial or not. Whether to go to Marian or not, he amended with a wry twist of his lips.

He snorted and reached for another saw to oil. He'd done it again. Fallen head over heels like a schoolboy for the wrong woman.

He'd thought after living under the same roof all these months and working in close proximity at the mission, he knew Marian. He'd thought her innocent, pure. . .and within the last year she'd been engaged not once but twice, and one of those times to a man she knew to be a criminal!

What was the matter with him? Had God set him on earth merely to be a whipping boy when it came to women?

Discovering Marian's engagement to Rasmus had hurt, hurt like fury, and after that he didn't dare trust her.

But then, she'd been hurt, too. Hurt by Justin, and Rasmus, and the fear of her actions becoming food for the gossipmongers of the society circles she frequented with Philander Paget.

The more he'd thought of the detailed coverage the Minneapolis and St. Paul newspapers gave such trials—lurid descriptions, making victims of those testifying as much as of the defendant—the more he'd known he had to be at her side, if she wanted him there. It would be gruesome for her, having the entire world—or at least all of Minnesota—hear of Justin's marriage to another while engaged to her, and of her subsequent engagement to Rasmus.

No matter that she'd as much as ripped his heart out and torn it to ribbons, he couldn't let her face that alone. And she would be alone, even with her family beside her. What she needed was someone else who had gone through losing trust in one in whom they had every reason to believe, and the pain of people snickering or pitying them.

He doubted there was anyone else in her life who would understand what she faced as well as he did. He'd have hated to have the details of his wife's abandonment and betrayal broadcast far and wide in the newspapers.

But he wasn't about to trust her. No matter what, he wasn't going to risk his and Aurelia's happiness again, certainly not with a woman who exhibited such unstable affections.

Now if he could just convince his heart to quit loving her.

He tossed down his cleaning cloth on the work table in disgust. His mind was going around in the same circle it had been ever since he'd heard of her engagement to Rasmus.

"Everything all right, Mr. Starr?"

Everett's head jerked up. He'd forgotten Jules. The boy-turning-young-man leaned on the long broom handle, staring soberly at him beneath the small bill of the biking hat he wore inside and out, regardless of the many times Everett had reminded him to remove it indoors.

"Everything's fine. Just tired, I guess."

"Saw the articles in the newspaper the last couple days 'bout the Rasmus Pierce trial." Hesitancy made the voice almost monotone.

"Could hardly help it."

"Yeah." The acknowledgement seemed to make him a degree more comfortable with the topic. "One of the people testifyin' is named Marian Ames."

Everett met his gaze evenly. "And?"

Jules shifted his feet and frowned. "Well, that wouldn't be yer Miss Ames, would it?"

Everett leaned a hip against the work table and tried to keep his voice impersonal. "She isn't *my* Miss Ames, but yes, it's the Miss Ames you've seen with my daughter, the young woman who assists with the free kindergarten at the mission."

"Sir, if ya don't mind me askin', me and the guys been wonderin' how a lady like that would get mixed up in such things? I mean, we seen lots a things on the streets, and we know not ever' lady is a lady, if ya get my meanin'."

"I get your meaning." His lips stretched so tautly his teeth hurt. Young boys making their living on the street grew up a whale too fast for their own good. He wished he could do a lot more for them than a weekly Sunday school session, a hot meal, and an occasional woodworking class, like he'd given them tonight.

"Well, it seems from the newspaper reports that the criminal's lawyer don't think much of Miss Ames. Any of us news rats could tell him she's a lady through and through. Why'd that lawyer try ta say she'd been engaged ta Rasmus?"

Everett gave his attention diligently to brushing minute bits of sawdust from the workbench. "It's his job to do everything he can to convince the jury his client's innocent. I guess he thought Rasmus couldn't be accused of kidnapping his own fiancée."

Jules rested his chin on top of the broom handle. "I dunno. Accordin' ta the papers, Rasmus forced that man and woman ta marry. Anyone could see the likes of Miss Ames wouldn't be engaged ta Rasmus Pierce of her own intentions."

The boy had more faith in Marian than he did, Everett thought, but then he didn't know the complete story. Even so, the boy's attitude shamed him somewhat.

"Well, the boys and me, we decided already that Miss Ames is true as they come, and we're not goin' ta believe anythin' we read in the papers that says otherwise." As if to emphasize his point, he went back to sweeping with a vigor.

"She'd be pleased to know it. Maybe you should send her a note saying so."

Color submerged the street-hardened young face. "Me, sir?" The squeak in his voice deepened the color.

Everett pretended not to notice his discomfort. He shrugged casually. "Not you in particular. I was thinking maybe the News-boys as a group could send it. A bit of encouragement when you're under the gun like Miss Ames is now means a lot."

Jules shuffled his feet. "Yeah. Well, I'll talk ta the boys 'bout it."

Most likely nothing will come of it, Everett thought. Maybe he should put a note in next time he helped Aurelia write her a letter, mentioning the boys' belief in her. Maybe it would make up a little for his own lack of faith.

But he wasn't going to let himself trust her.

❧

Marian closed Aunt Dorothy's front door behind the hackman

who had carried in her trunk and bags. She drew off her gloves and laid them on the inlaid hall table, listening intently. Nothing, no sound at all.

A quick tour of the house convinced her no one was home. Likely Aunt Dorothy, Aurelia, and Everett were at the mission. Sonja and Anna were probably at the market. Her heart slowly resumed its normal rhythm when she knew she wouldn't be seeing Everett momentarily.

At least she knew from Aurelia's and Aunt Dorothy's notes that Everett and Aurelia hadn't moved elsewhere. She tried not to hope their presence in the house meant he was ready to let himself love her.

To lift her spirits, she changed from her traveling suit into a pink organdy gown trimmed with delightfully intricate lacework. Her mother had insisted on purchasing her a new spring gown and accessories before she returned to Minneapolis, and Marian was glad now that she had.

The hall clock bonged a laborious two o'clock while she descended the stairway, and with a sudden determination, she retrieved from the trunk still standing in the hall the matching new hat with its fashionably wide brim, and her lace-and-flower-bedecked parasol. It was too late to go to the mission this afternoon, and she was too restless to stay about the house alone. A beautiful sunshiny day in May shouldn't be wasted; she'd visit Minnehaha.

When she'd been home, she'd visited the river every evening. She found it comforting to be near the river that flowed over the Falls of St. Anthony near the mission and those she loved in Minneapolis. The ribbon of water was a tangible connection to Everett.

She lifted her gown's fragile material carefully out of the way of the rough-hewn stairs leading down the bluff into the valley below the falls. Anticipation at seeing the celebrated waterfall again made the birds' songs sweeter and the new leaves greener. The invigorating smells of fresh earth, new spring growth, and refreshing spring waters surrounded her. Large woods violets lifted their deeply colored heads joyfully at the edge of the stairs and peeked around the roots of trees at the clearing's edge.

There were only a handful of others to share the beauty with her today, doubtless because it was the middle of a weekday afternoon. A couple of about thirty stood in the midst of the bridge, admiring the veil of white water falling straight and true to the creek below, each holding a pudgy hand of their toddling, curly-topped daughter between them. Two boys with shocks of red hair and freckle-covered cheeks, looking remarkably alike, climbed over and under the logs crisscrossing below the railing. Their laughter and challenges to each other rang through the quiet glen.

Settling herself on the wooden bench at the edge of the clearing, she smiled softly, the ache that was becoming depressingly familiar starting in her chest. Such an atmosphere of contentment hung about the young family! In unguarded moments, she'd daydreamed of herself and Everett raising such a family. He was a marvelous father to Aurelia. She knew from his devotion to the Newsboys that he'd love having sons.

She shouldn't allow herself to think of such things. Everett's sacrifice in coming to her side during the trial was more than she'd had any right to expect. It was selfish to wish for more.

Everett had been worried at the pain the revelation of her broken engagement to Justin, and her engagement to Rasmus would bring her. She hadn't the courage to tell him no pain could be worse than losing him from her life.

The glen was quieter after the family left. Squirrels darted about, rustling in the underbrush, twitching their tails while studying her from the safety of a branch or fallen log. Birds hopped along the branches and beneath bushes, searching for a stray seed or careless insect. The purl of the waterfall sang through the narrow, greening valley.

She made her way slowly toward the middle of the bridge, and once there, hooked the edge of her lacy parasol over the railing beside her. Her gaze studied the wooded banks, the draft of cool air caused by the falling water refreshing against her cheeks.

Longfellow would have us believe Hiawatha came here to claim his bride, she thought. It was a lovely piece of a sad story, but it wasn't true, any more than her dream that Everett would claim her heart.

That didn't remove the beauty God had created in this almost hidden valley. It was achingly lovely. She was glad it was Everett and Aurelia who had introduced her to it.

The crack of a twig sounded unnatural among the scurrying and exploring whispers of the small glen animals and birds, and it caught Marian's attention. She turned toward it, curious, and froze with one hand on the railing.

Everett! Why was he standing at the edge of the wild area through which they'd traversed to Minnegiggle? He should be at the mission.

Her presence must have surprised him just as much, for he was as still as she, their gazes questioning each other across the small clearing.

He slipped his favorite, comfortable slouch hat slowly from his head, mussing slightly the hair which the sun dappled with bright strands through the oak leaves. A small smile touched her lips, recalling the stiff gray derby he'd purchased to accompany her to the trial.

Her heart beat faster at every step that brought him closer, until he stopped within a foot of her, and the sound hid the cascading falls from her ears.

"I couldn't believe it was you."

"Nor I you." She spoke around the pulse fluttering in her throat.

His gaze swept over her dress and back to her face. "You're beautiful."

A number of men had said those words to her before, but never had they meant so much.

"I read in this morning's *Tribune* that the trial is over, but I didn't expect you back so soon."

Had he expected her back today, would he and Aurelia have left Aunt Dorothy's for good before she arrived? She didn't want to know yet. "Rasmus was found guilty."

"Guess there was never any doubt of that."

She watched her string-gloved index finger trace a split in the railing. "He. . .he told me it was his affection for me that resulted in his apprehension."

"If it weren't for the crimes he chose to commit, no one would have sought to apprehend him. It's his own fault he's in prison, not yours."

She nodded, still watching the restless finger.

She told him of urging Rasmus to seek the Lord. She met his gaze. "He wasn't required to lie to the court about our engagement."

"No, he wasn't. We'll keep praying for him."

We?

She took a deep breath and plunged into what she'd wanted to say to him for so long, her words tripping over each other almost as quickly as the water danced on the rocks below the falls. "I was such a child when my engagement to Justin was broken and I became engaged to Rasmus. I acted willful and silly, trying to work revenge against Justin."

"I tried to convince myself of that very thing," he admitted gruffly, his gaze searching the waters flowing beneath them. "I kept telling myself you were foolish and nothing but trouble, that you couldn't be trusted."

She held her breath, almost afraid to hear what he was saying.

He reached for her hands, and she hoped he wouldn't notice she was trembling from the top of her new, lace-covered bonnet to the tips of her toes. "Perhaps you didn't act wisely when you found out about Justin and Constance."

"Perhaps?"

The twinkle that jumped to his eyes sent a thrill of relief shimmering through her.

"All right, so there's no perhaps about it." His smile faded. "The fact is, we all do foolish things in our lives; a lot of foolish things, in spite of the firmest resolve. You had more incentive than most of us for your actions. Your engagement to Justin gave you every reason to trust his loyalty implicitly. It's natural you lashed out at Justin in the manner you thought would most hurt him."

"That didn't make it right."

"No, it didn't, but it's understandable. I should have understood more than most people, after what my wife put me and Aurelia through. I know all about betrayal by the one person you believe loves you more than life. It eats through your gut like acid."

This was her opportunity to tell him her reasons for not sharing everything about her past sooner. Her pulse raced at the thought. It would be very bold to do so.

He still held her hands, playing his broad thumbs over the backs of her gloves, nicks in his work-worn skin tugging gently at the strings. His touch gave her courage.

"I was terrified you would despise me if you found out about Rasmus. You and Aurelia have become. . .important to me. I didn't wish to lose your friendship."

He squeezed her hands. "If I'd waited to hear your complete explanation instead of storming off in a rage the morning you told me about Rasmus, perhaps I wouldn't have reacted so badly. I didn't want to let myself trust you. I didn't want to be hurt again. I'm sorry."

His gruff apology was like a gift from heaven.

"One of the things that amazed me about you from the beginning was your sweet, joyous spirit. The first time I heard your voice and looked into your eyes, I thought of Minnehaha, 'Laughing Water.' I thought you must be innocent, unexposed to the cruelties the world can dish out. Then you told me about Justin, and I knew I was wrong. Your lack of bitterness fascinated me, because I was letting bitterness warp my life."

A smile grew in the depths of the brown eyes she loved before he continued. "I've watched you with Aurelia, and with the kindergarten children. I've seen your devotion to the free kindergarten and its cause, and the way you've thrown your energy into the numerous efforts to help the unemployed, especially the Swedish people in our neighborhood." His thumb brushed a loose tendril from her cheek, sending delightful shivers through her. "You're no longer a child, in any manner."

The deep timbre in his voice set her pulses quick-stepping, and she moved back slightly, nervous. He kept hold of her hands and his smile challenged her to stay where she was. "I've loved you for months, but I was afraid to trust again. I finally realized I could chance the possibility of being hurt by love, or I could live with the certain pain of a life without trust, a life without you."

He loved her!

"May I court you?"

"Court me?" Her eyes widened in surprise and she heard the dismay in her own voice.

The confident joy in his eyes faded, routed by disappointment. *So it wasn't to be,* he thought grimly. Well, he wasn't sorry he'd asked. If he hadn't, he'd always have wondered whether he'd had a chance with her.

He should drop her hands, but she hadn't tugged at them, and he dreaded giving up this last touch with her.

"I'm sure it would be delightful to be courted by you, but," she hesitated, and he searched her eyes guardedly.

"But?"

"I was rather hoping you would ask me to be your wife instead."

Joy flowed over him as wildly as the Mississippi over its banks during a spring flood. He crushed her to him exultantly. "Marian!"

"Oh!" She grasped her wide-brimmed hat, knocked askew in his exuberance.

He stood impatiently watching her make repairs to her outfit, noting with pleasure the rosy color that tinged her cheeks, and the shy joy that shone in the eyes that would meet his for a moment, then skitter away.

His gaze drifted over her filmy pink dress, and his joy began to ebb away.

When she'd secured the hat, he reached to touch one of the gauzy sleeves tentatively. "I wouldn't be able to buy you gowns like this."

Her gaze didn't dart away this time. "Then I shan't ask you to do so."

"You'll miss the parties and outings."

"I'd miss you more."

"I'll never be able to offer you everything men like Justin Knight and Philander Paget can offer."

He watched a smile quiver at the edge of her lips, and restrained with difficulty his desire to kiss her there.

"Are you refusing me, Mr. Starr?"

"I want to be certain you know what you'll be receiving."

"I'm certain." She caught her hands behind her and looked about with a teasing nonchalance which delighted him. "Well, you know what Sonja's grandmother says."

"What does she say this time?"

"'When our Lord gives, one should keep the sack open.' So why are you closing yours?"

His laughter spilled out. He opened his arms to her with all reservations gone, and she moved into them with an eagerness which left him feeling humble.

"Will you be my wife?"

Her slender arms tightened about his neck. "Yes, a thousand times and forever, yes!"

Wonder and thanksgiving flooded his chest to think his love caused the joy filling her eyes. "Remember these lines from *Hiawatha*? 'Love is sunshine, hate is shadow. . .rule by love.' You gave me the desire to let God's love rule in my life again, instead of anger and bitterness."

Her fingers rested lightly against his cheeks. "Our life together will always be ruled by love."

Healing slipped sweet peace around his heart at the promise in her eyes and words.

"I love you," he whispered against her lips.

Minnehaha laughed sweetly in the background, reflecting the joy in their hearts.

A Letter To Our Readers

Dear Reader:

In order that we might better contribute to your reading enjoyment, we would appreciate your taking a few minutes to respond to the following questions. When completed, please return to the following:

Rebecca Germany, Editor
Heartsong Presents
P.O. Box 719
Uhrichsville, Ohio 44683

1. Did you enjoy reading *Rekindled Flame*?
   ❑ Very much. I would like to see more books
      by this author!
   ❑ Moderately
      I would have enjoyed it more if _____

   _____

2. Are you a member of *Heartsong Presents*? Yes   No
   If no, where did you purchase this book? _____

   _____

3. What influenced your decision to purchase this
   book? (Check those that apply.)

   ❑ Cover   ❑ Back cover copy

   ❑ Title   ❑ Friends

   ❑ Publicity   ❑ Other _____

4. On a scale from 1 (poor) to 10 (superior), please rate the following elements.

    ___Heroine   ___Plot

    ___Hero   ___Inspirational theme

    ___Setting   ___Secondary characters

5. What settings would you like to see covered in *Heartsong Presents* books?

_____

_____

6. What are some inspirational themes you would like to see treated in future books?_____

_____

_____

7. Would you be interested in reading other *Heartsong Presents* titles?   ❑ Yes   ❑ No

8. Please check your age range:
❑ Under 18   ❑ 18-24   ❑ 25-34
❑ 35-45   ❑ 46-55   ❑ Over 55

9. How many hours per week do you read? ————

Name _____

Occupation _____

Address _____

City _____ State _____ Zip _____

JoAnn A. Grote

__*The Sure Promise*—Haunted by her own lonely childhood, Laurina Dalen is determined to provide a home for the Wells children. Matthew Strong is determined to meet the medical needs of the prairie dwellers. Laurina and Matthew belong to the prairie. . .but first they must belong to each other. HP36

__*The Unfolding Heart*—As Millicent and Adam's attraction for each other grows, Millicent realizes she could never make a good wife for a minister. And even if she could, how could she ever bring herself to live with him amid the crudeness and danger of the frontier? HP51

__*Treasure of the Heart*—John Wells leaves his fiancée in Minnesota to go in search of the reason for his father's murder. Among the Black Hills of South Dakota he finds the answers he needs, as well as a rare treasure of the heart, Jewell Emerson. HP55

__*Love's Shining Hope*—As Pearl and Jason are drawn closer together in the worst of times, Pearl is faced with a decision like no other. Should she accept Jason's hasty proposal, well aware that he wants a marriage in name only to run the farm? HP103

__*An Honest Love*—Constance Ward's work as a Pinkerton agent requires secrecy and deception. Little does she realize that she will also be required to marry a total stranger. Joined before God under circumstances of fear and falsehood, Constance and Justin Knight struggle to accept each other without the benefit of loving trust. HP103

Hearts♥ng

HISTORICAL ROMANCE IS CHEAPER BY THE DOZEN!

Any 12 *Heartsong Presents* titles for only $26.95 *

Buy any assortment of twelve *Heartsong Presents* titles and save 25% off of the already discounted price of $2.95 each!

*plus $1.00 shipping and handling per order and sales tax where applicable.

HEARTSONG PRESENTS TITLES AVAILABLE NOW:

__HP 1 TORCH FOR TRINITY, *Colleen L. Reece*＊
__HP 2 WILDFLOWER HARVEST, *Colleen L. Reece*＊
__HP 7 CANDLESHINE, *Colleen L. Reece*
__HP 8 DESERT ROSE, *Colleen L. Reece*
__HP 11 RIVER OF FIRE, *Jacquelyn Cook*＊
__HP 12 COTTONWOOD DREAMS, *Norene Morris*＊
__HP 15 WHISPERS ON THE WIND, *Maryn Langer*
__HP 16 SILENCE IN THE SAGE, *Colleen L. Reece*
__HP 19 A PLACE TO BELONG, *Janelle Jamison*＊
__HP 20 SHORES OF PROMISE, *Kate Blackwell*＊
__HP 23 GONE WEST, *Kathleen Karr*
__HP 24 WHISPERS IN THE WILDERNESS, *Colleen L. Reece*
__HP 27 BEYOND THE SEARCHING RIVER, *Jacquelyn Cook*
__HP 28 DAKOTA DAWN, *Lauraine Snelling*
__HP 31 DREAM SPINNER, *Sally Laity*
__HP 32 THE PROMISED LAND, *Kathleen Karr*
__HP 35 WHEN COMES THE DAWN, *Brenda Bancroft*
__HP 36 THE SURE PROMISE, *JoAnn A. Grote*
__HP 39 RAINBOW HARVEST, *Norene Morris*
__HP 40 PERFECT LOVE, *Janelle Jamison*
__HP 43 VEILED JOY, *Colleen L. Reece*
__HP 44 DAKOTA DREAM, *Lauraine Snelling*
__HP 47 TENDER JOURNEYS, *Janelle Jamison*
__HP 48 SHORES OF DELIVERANCE, *Kate Blackwell*
__HP 51 THE UNFOLDING HEART, *JoAnn A. Grote*
__HP 52 TAPESTRY OF TAMAR, *Colleen L. Reece*
__HP 55 TREASURE OF THE HEART, *JoAnn A. Grote*
__HP 56 A LIGHT IN THE WINDOW, *Janelle Jamison*
__HP 59 EYES OF THE HEART, *Maryn Langer*
__HP 60 MORE THAN CONQUERORS, *Kay Cornelius*
__HP 63 THE WILLING HEART, *Janelle Jamison*
__HP 64 CROWS'-NESTS AND MIRRORS, *Colleen L. Reece*
__HP 67 DAKOTA DUSK, *Lauraine Snelling*
__HP 68 RIVERS RUSHING TO THE SEA, *Jacquelyn Cook*
__HP 71 DESTINY'S ROAD, *Janelle Jamison*
__HP 72 SONG OF CAPTIVITY, *Linda Herring*
__HP 75 MUSIC IN THE MOUNTAINS, *Colleen L. Reece*
__HP 76 HEARTBREAK TRAIL, *VeraLee Wiggins*   ＊Temporarily out of stock.

(If ordering from this page, please remember to include it with the order form.)

··········Presents··········

*Temporarily out of stock.

Great Inspirational Romance at a Great Price!

Heartsong Presents books are inspirational romances in contemporary and historical settings, designed to give you an enjoyable, spirit-lifting reading experience. You can choose from 136 wonderfully written titles from some of today's best authors like Colleen L. Reece, Brenda Bancroft, Janelle Jamison, and many others.

When ordering quantities less than twelve, above titles are $2.95 each.

Hearts♥ng Presents
Love Stories Are Rated G!

That's for godly, gratifying, and of course, great! If you love a thrilling love story, but don't appreciate the sordidness of popular paperback romances, **Heartsong Presents** is for you. In fact, **Heartsong Presents** is the *only inspirational romance book club*, the only one featuring love stories where Christian faith is the primary ingredient in a marriage relationship.

Sign up today to receive your first set of four, never before published Christian romances. Send no money now; you will receive a bill with the first shipment. You may cancel at any time without obligation, and if you aren't completely satisfied with any selection, you may return the books for an immediate refund!

Imagine. . .four new romances every month—two historical, two contemporary—with men and women like you who long to meet the one God has chosen as the love of their lives. . .all for the low price of $9.97 postpaid.

To join, simply complete the coupon below and mail to the address provided. **Heartsong Presents** romances are rated G for another reason: They'll arrive *Godspeed!*
